SWEET
MASTERPIECE

Connie Shelton

Books by Connie Shelton

THE CHARLIE PARKER MYSTERY SERIES

THE SAMANTHA SWEET MYSTERY SERIES

CHILDREN'S BOOKS

SWEET

MASTERPIECE

The First Samantha Sweet Mystery

Connie Shelton

Secret Staircase Books

Sweet Masterpiece
Published by Secret Staircase Books, an imprint of
Columbine Publishing Group
PO Box 416, Angel Fire, NM 87710

Printed and bound in the United States of America
ISBN 1945422009
ISBN-13 9781945422003

This book is a work of fiction. Names, characters, places and
incidents are either the product of the author's imagination or are
used fictitiously. Any resemblance to actual events or locales or
persons, living or dead, is entirely coincidental. Although the author
and publisher have made every effort to ensure the accuracy and
completeness of information contained in this book we assume
no responsibility for errors, inaccuracies, omissions, or any
inconsistency herein. Any slights of people, places or organizations
are unintentional.

Book layout and design by Secret Staircase Books
Cover illustration © Robertas Pezas
Cover cupcake design © Makeitdoubleplz

First trade paperback edition: September, 2010
Also published in e-book editions: August, 2010

Fiction Categories:
Mystery/Female Sleuth/Romantic Suspense
/Paranormal Mystery

To Dan, always. I am your #1 fan.

And to Susan, Serena and the Writers Guild members who have been so supportive and helpful in all my endeavors.

Mostly, to all my loyal readers over the years. I couldn't have done it without you!

Chapter 1

Chocolate icing shot out of the pastry bag as Samantha Sweet tested the consistency of her newest batch. The ridges held shape. Perfect. She picked up a triple-chocolate Kahlua cupcake and proceeded to pipe a thick base of chocolate buttercream on it. On top of that, a smaller cone, which she built up then tapered to form a snout. Two perky ears. Switching to a small round tip she quickly added short fur and watched as the cupcake became a shaggy puppy's head. White chocolate eyes with dark chocolate irises. White chocolate tinted pink for its tiny tongue.

Sam smiled at the happy little face she had created. Set him down and started another. The order was for the Tuesday night book group and local chapter of Chocoholics Unanimous. Every detail, right down to the dogs' collars, had to be chocolate, and Sam enjoyed matching the theme of the weekly treats to that of the book they were reading, in this case a story featuring a dog walker. Unlike typical 'anonymous' twelve-step groups, this bunch celebrated their addiction. They reveled in the utter enjoyment of all things chocolate. There was absolutely no intention of overcoming their mutual habit. Sam wasn't complaining—the weekly order gave a nice boost to her fledgling little home business. And someday . . . a shop . . . Sweet's Sweets.

She added the final touches to a schnauzer, then covered the bowl of chocolate cream and put it in the fridge. Chided herself as she licked a gob of the frosting from her finger— where did she think those extra pounds came from? She ran hot water and detergent into a bowl and tossed all the implements into it to soak until she could get back.

She had to break into a house and she was running late.

Sam rechecked the address, debated hitching up her utility trailer and decided against it. This wasn't supposed to be that big a job. The pickup should handle it fine.

The house turned out to be a flat-roofed adobe with traditional two-foot-thick walls, on the south side of Taos. She backed into the driveway, a long one that led to the back of the place. Getting out, she circled the whole house, checking doors and windows for anything inadvertently left open. She couldn't remember how many times she'd gone to a huge effort to pick a lock or drill a deadbolt, just to find out that the back door was unlocked all along. Talk about frustrating.

No such luck this time. The traditional blue-painted doors were all buttoned up tight. She pulled out her tool bag and analyzed the lock on the back door. They were almost always less beefy than front doors, for some stupid reason. And that held true at this place. Rather than drill the lock, which then required that she replace it before leaving, she decided to see if she could pick this one. One of these days she would see about getting one of those little triggered pick guns, but at the moment all she could afford were standard picks, which take two hands and a lot of patience to operate. It was nothing like it looked in the movies, she quickly discovered when she began this line of work.

She worked the picks for close to five minutes before feeling the telltale release of the tumblers. Blew out a breath. That was another part of success at this—seemed like you had to be holding your breath to make it work. She grabbed the doorknob and got that tweaky feeling in the gut, that uncertain what-lies-behind-this-door question, each time she entered a strange house.

She'd envisioned a recalcitrant homeowner, refusing to leave, shotgun in hand, or maybe a wall-high stack of newspapers ready to topple onto her. Everyone's read about some weird old man who had a house full of them. But none of that had happened to her, yet.

Breaking into houses for a living—all perfectly legal and sanctioned by the U.S. government. The USDA hired folks like Samantha to clean and maintain abandoned properties where the homeowner defaulted on their loans. Sadly, there were a lot of them these days.

She noticed that a thin crust of dirt covered the door and all the glass panes on this side of the house, remnants of New Mexico's famous "mud storms" where blowing dirt and a small amount of rain combined to coat every surface with a haze of brown. Sam actually liked this part of the job, assessing the situation and imagining how good it would look after she'd applied Windex and hot water. The knob twisted in her hand and the door swung open with a hellish creak. A little oil would take care of that. She brushed her hands on her jeans and stuffed the lock tools back into her canvas bag, leaving it sitting just inside the back door. Flipped on the lights. At least the power had not been cut yet.

Here's where the surprises usually showed up. In this case the kitchen was remarkably untrashed—sometimes kitchens were a nightmare. A few crusted dishes sat in the sink but the table was clear, trashcan still had its top firmly in place, and no roaches scurried away. No noxious odors from the fridge. She would come back to that.

She walked through a doorway into a living/dining L and saw that the home still contained furniture. Three doors opened off a short hallway—a little pink bathroom was visible but the other two doors were closed. A starter home for a young family, certainly adequate for a retired couple. She'd seen quite a few similar, and it wasn't a whole lot smaller than her own place on Elmwood Lane.

In the living room an ancient sofa looked like prime real estate for dust mites and a round coffee table held several red pillar candles with hard wax drips down their sides. Dusty-looking bundles of dried herbs lay among the candles, and an open book sat on the sofa, as if the reader had simply gotten up in mid-chapter and planned to return. The rest of the room was cluttered with a lifetime's accumulation—shelves held stacks of magazines and cheaply framed photos of children in 1940s attire. An old fashioned wooden radio had cobwebs lacing its speaker and trailing between the knobs.

Sam wandered through the room, trailing her fingers across the fringe on the shade of an old floor lamp. Then she heard a thump.

The hair on her neck rose. *I'm getting too old for this.*

She searched for a weapon of any kind. The floor lamp looked heavy but completely unwieldy. She edged back to the kitchen and pulled the biggest wrench, a crescent only ten inches long, from her tool kit.

"Hello?" she called out.

The thump came a tiny bit louder this time.

"Hello? USDA caretaker. Anyone here?" She tiptoed into the hallway, her steps silent on the worn saltillo tile.

This time she swore she heard a moan. No way this could be a good thing. She should call 911, she thought, even as she reached out to the first closed bedroom door and turned the knob.

The smell of illness and old-person emanated from the room as soon as the door opened. Sam held her breath for a moment. The place was so dim she had a hard time finding the source of the sound. A wooden bed took up most of the space, while a high dresser on the far wall and a nightstand cluttered with bottles, drinking glasses and wadded tissues filled the rest of the space. Crumpled blankets created waves on the surface of the bed and it took her a moment to realize that a tiny, shriveled woman lay under them.

Another moan, barely above a whisper.

"Ma'am?"

A thin hand fluttered upward. Sam stepped closer to the bedside.

"I'm sent here by the USDA," she said. "I'm supposed to clean up the house, but I'm sure they didn't realize anyone was living here."

The toothless mouth opened and a sound emerged, something like a piece of cellophane being crushed and then ripped. The old woman wiped at her forehead and made some more throat-clearing noises. Finally, words emerged. "Not . . . for . . . long."

"What? Can I do something for you?" Sam reached for one of the water glasses on the nightstand but the clawlike hand waved her away.

"I have . . . something . . ."

Sam leaned in a little closer, and the woman cleared her throat noisily. She jammed a tissue at the scrawny fingers and stepped back. When the woman spoke again her voice was noticeably stronger.

"I have something for you," she said.

"I don't think you even know me, ma'am."

The birdlike woman raised up on one elbow and her tiny eyes lost their blurry look for a moment. "I know . . . you were meant to come here . . . today. You are to possess the secret."

What on earth did *that* mean?

She fell back against her pillows, clearly tired from the effort.

"Quickly, girl. The bottom . . . drawer . . . in the dresser."

"You need something from the dresser." Sam turned toward it.

"A wooden box. Bottom drawer . . . look . . . under . . ."

Sam went over to the dresser, stooped clumsily, and fumbled at the cheap brass handles, pulling it open. It seemed to be stuffed full of cloth—bedding, knitted items and such.

"Get . . . the . . . box. Under—" The words caught in her throat.

Sam glanced up at the sick woman. She lay against the pillow, eyes closed, breathing shallowly through her mouth. Sam dug through the fabric, feeling for anything that might be the box she wanted. In the back left corner she felt a hard surface and pulled at it.

It was about the size of a cigar box, with a crude metal clasp and a lumpy, carved surface. She picked it up and went back to the old woman's side.

"Here you go. Here's your box."

The eyelids fluttered but didn't really open. "No . . . for you."

"Me? Are you sure?"

From somewhere deep inside, the ancient woman called up the strength to raise her head again. "The box has . . . special powers. It holds . . . many truths."

Sam stared at the ugly, lumpy thing. "What's in it?"

The old head fell back to the pillow. "Quickly . . . take it. Put it in a safe place."

Sam stood there, uncertainly, wondering what the woman was telling her.

"Now, girl. Take it." A labored breath. "No one must know."

The lady needed medical attention but the poor thing wouldn't be satisfied until she thought Sam had taken the box to a safe place.

"I'm going to call an ambulance for you. I'll put this in my truck for safe keeping." Sam's voice shook, worried that the woman would go into cardiac arrest at any second.

The pained expression on the old woman's face relaxed. The answer seemed to satisfy her.

"Okay, just rest. I'll have some help here for you soon." Sam patted the woman's shoulder, shocked to feel sharp

Chapter 2

In her fifty-two years, Sam had never been alone with someone recently deceased and standing by the bed gave her the willies. She stepped outside and dialed her USDA contracting officer's number. She'd never met Delbert Crow in person but she imagined a gray-haired fussy bureaucrat who was a year or two from retirement. At times he was so by-the-book that he drove her crazy with details; other times she got the impression he didn't want to be bothered, that he couldn't wait to be out on his fishing boat on a lake a hundred miles from nowhere. Somehow she had a feeling that finding a dying woman at one of her properties would be something he'd want to know about.

"Have you called the police?" he asked.

"The Sheriff's Department, actually. We're just outside the town limits here. Well, I just dialed 911 and—"

"Fine, fine." She heard papers rustling, as if he were

looking in the procedures manual for an answer. What could this be listed under—discovery of dead body on premises? "Ms. Sweet, it will be all right. Just wait there until the authorities arrive. I'm sure they can handle it. If the sheriff needs to speak to me, I'm at my office all day."

Sam paced the front porch, unable to make herself go back into the house with the dead woman. A Sheriff's Department SUV, an ambulance and a private car arrived within minutes of each other. The man in the private car introduced himself as the county's Field Deputy Medical Investigator before he bustled into the house.

The lean guy who unfolded himself out of the SUV walked over to her. "Ms. Sweet? Deputy Sheriff Beau Cardwell." There was definite Southern in the accent and the way he said her name made it sound like an invitation to dance a waltz. The last guy she knew named Beau was way back in her teen years in Texas, but that was a whole other story involving a girl with lusty hormones and a football player whose kiss would send any good girl off the deep end. She firmly shut *that* image out of her head.

The deputy was staring at her.

Awkward moment. "Uh, yes. I'm Samantha Sweet. Just call me Sam."

He sent a lopsided grin her way, as if he'd just read her mind.

"Okay. Sam." He cleared his throat and flipped open a small notebook.

At the back of the ambulance, two EMTs snapped on latex gloves and yanked out a gurney, which they wheeled toward the house.

"The mortgage on the house was government guaranteed and was in foreclosure," Sam told the deputy.

She gave the basics of how she'd gotten inside. She told him the old woman had spoken to her very briefly and died while she'd stepped outside to summon medical help for her. Remembering the woman's warning, she didn't mention the wooden box although she felt a little funny about that.

"Do you know who she was?" Sam asked.

"Bertha Martinez. She lived alone." He scratched notes as he talked. "We think there's a grandson in Albuquerque. He may have been the one who talked her into signing a mortgage to get some cash out of the property. Can't imagine why she would have done it otherwise. Place has been in her family for a couple hundred years. She refused to go to a care home when her neighbors recommended it. I'd been out here several times, but never could convince her. Last five years or so she used to chase me off. Met me on the porch with a shotgun a couple times."

"Really?"

"Yeah. A real sad thing. Local stories ran wild. Some say she was a witch, some just held that she was crazy. Got old and sick but never would see a doctor. Just wanted to be left alone, I guess."

"USDA sends me to clean out abandoned places so they can be sold. I've never had one where anyone was still living in the house. I'm sure they thought she'd moved away or already died."

He wrote on his forms, filling out the address of the property and noting what she'd just told him.

The M.I. came out of the house, stuffing his stethoscope into the black bag he carried. "Natural causes, old age," he said. "Albuquerque OMI will confirm that and issue the death certificate at the morgue." He got into his vehicle and drove away.

"So, what should I do?" Sam asked Deputy Cardwell. "Ordinarily, the owners have taken away whatever they want and I just clean the place up."

"Can it wait a day or two? Give us time to remove the body, do a quick check of the house to be sure nothing's out of order. Make one more run at finding the grandson. Maybe you could come back on Thursday?"

"Sure, no problem. I'll leave a sign-in sheet on the kitchen counter. Anyone who comes in is supposed to sign it and state what they're doing here." She hoped following that bit of protocol would satisfy Delbert Crow.

Cardwell didn't look especially happy about complying but he nodded.

She retrieved her tool kit from the kitchen, found a house key in a dish near the front door and, after verifying that it worked in the lock, placed it in a lockbox and went out to her red Silverado.

The day was still young—not quite noon. Sam drove through town, past Wal-Mart and the movie theater and turned right on Kit Carson Road, at the plaza. Zigzagged a couple of blocks south and east to her little lane. Her house felt cool under the shade of the huge cottonwoods that grew everywhere in this part of Taos. She went into the bathroom and washed her face and hands thoroughly, eager to rid herself of the morning's disturbing experience. A brush taken to her hair only made the graying, short layers stick out in all directions with static electricity. Giving up on that, she went to the kitchen and made a quick sandwich from leftover ham and decided she could still earn a little money today, even though one of her jobs was on hold.

She grabbed the wide platter of chocolate puppy-dog cupcakes she'd made earlier and headed out to Mysterious

Happenings, the bookstore where the Chocoholics group met to solve mysteries, and gorge. They liked to choose a mystery novel, read up to the final chapter, and then meet to guess at the ending. They read the ending of the book together and then there was some kind of prize for whoever came closest to figuring it out. One of the members, a British born little slip of a thing, always seemed to come away with either the prize for eating the biggest quantity of the evening's chocolate treats or for figuring out the mystery. As a female who had always carried about thirty pounds more than she wanted, Sam had no idea how Riki managed to stay barely above the weight of a Doberman.

A bell tinkled over the bookshop door when she entered, balancing the tray of cupcakes and squeezing past a display rack of jigsaw puzzles.

"Madame Samantha!" The bookshop owner, Ivan Petrenko, spread his arms wide and stepped from behind the counter. "Is looking most fabulous today!"

When he made statements like that, Sam was never sure if the flirtatious man was talking about the cupcakes or her.

She held up the tray. "Dogs. To go with this week's theme."

"*Da*, how *tres bien!*" Ivan's curious mixture of English, French and Russian came—according to local legend—from the fact that he'd defected from the Soviet Union with his wife's ballet troupe on a trip to Paris. The more outrageous versions of the story held that he'd worked in a diamond mine, apprenticed with a Cordon Bleu chef, waited tables in New York and finally come to New Mexico where he'd opened the bookshop ten years ago. As far as a timeframe for all this, Sam had no idea. He looked about forty, but that was a lot of living to cram into those few years. Although skeptical about a lot of Ivan's story, she had to admit that he was a colorful guy.

"Thanks, Ivan," she said as he handed her the check for the cupcakes. "Another treat for next week?"

"*Absolutement*. Using your judgment, please."

She left the shop, careful to hide the fact that she was nearly laughing aloud.

Next on her list was a property north and west of town, somewhere off Highway 64 toward the little crossroads town of Tres Piedras. Her paperwork mentioned that the place might need mowing, so she stopped back by her house and hitched up her utility trailer with lawn mower and the assortment of rakes, hoes and other gardening tools that were a requirement for a lot of these abandoned properties. She cruised through town and found the place about twenty minutes later, where a collection of a half-dozen small homes sat on plots of scrubby land, no more than an acre apiece.

A short drive led to the weathered wood frame house, which she entered by drilling the lock. No messing with picks on this one—she had a spare lockset in the trailer and it was a lot quicker this way. Replacing the damaged lock took only a few minutes.

This place was clearly abandoned, for which she was glad, after this morning's surprise. Although some pieces of furniture remained and there were papers and junk everywhere, the rooms had that hollow feel and neutral smell of a place that hadn't seen human habitation in awhile. Lucky me, she thought. Sometimes the first thing that hit when she walked in the door was eau de rotten meat, especially in a place where the fridge was full and the power had been cut off.

Although the kitchen was messy, the power was still on—probably an oversight by the rural co-op—and a glance in the fridge revealed that it was empty but for a ketchup bottle and a chunk of fuzzy blue-green cheese.

Sam put the requisite sign-in sheet in the kitchen and spent a few minutes making a list of projects: gather trash, sort possessions, then start cleaning. She could probably fit the trash in her truck and trailer, avoiding the need to hire a rolloff. At the back door she scanned the yard. The half-acre property had mainly been left wild, native sage dominating. But someone had gone to the trouble of planting grass around the house, and there were flower beds against the walls, a garden of sorts. An ancient swing set, rusty and obviously unused, sat in the middle of the grassy area, and she could tell that one of her first duties would be to mow. The stuff was a foot tall in places.

A glance at the sky revealed clouds towering in the distance, over Taos Mountain. The area would likely be in for a shower, which might vary from a few sprinkles to a full-fledged downpour. Since lightning could also be a factor it would be smart to attend to the mowing first.

Back at the pickup truck and utility trailer that she'd left out front, Sam unloaded the lawn mower, topped off the gas, and rolled it to the back. Bless it, the mower started on the first pull and she worked her way across the yard, finding her zone, taking pleasure in the neat rows of cut grass in her wake. It wasn't until she reached the far north edge of the grassy area that she realized part of the lawn was missing. Bare earth rose in a hump. A glint of white paint caught her eye and she stopped the mower. At one end of the mounded earth stood a small wooden cross with no markings. She walked over to it. A grave.

Chapter 3

The hair on her arms rose. Curious. And spooky.

According to the paperwork the owner, Mr. Riley Anderson, had abandoned the house less than six months ago. To Sam, the grave didn't look much older than that. What sad or morbid secrets had Anderson left behind?

Lightning cracked, no more than a mile away and Sam scurried to steer the mower under the protective cover of the carport beside the house. A thousand thoughts crowded her head, not the least of which was: What the hell! She had no idea whether a grave on private property was legal or not but figured she better report it.

As the first large raindrops splatted on the driveway, she pulled her cell phone from her jeans pocket and dialed.

"Delbert? Sam, again. You're not going to believe this."

He clearly didn't want to deal with any more dramatics. After listening to several longsuffering sighs, she suggested that he not worry about it—she would call the authorities, herself. Again.

The 911 operator, after hearing her fuzzy description of what she'd found, didn't seem to consider it a true emergency—as in the lights-and-sirens variety—but she did connect Sam with Sheriff Orlando Padilla's office.

Sam repeated her explanation about the gravesite and asked whether the sheriff might want to take a look.

"Sorry, he's out on a call," the dispatcher said. "Can you hold for a minute?"

Sam held, watching fat raindrops as they picked up speed, plopping off the hood of her truck, filling the air with the scent of wet dust.

The dispatcher's voice came back on the line. "I tried both radio and his cell phone, but he's up in the ski valley, probably out of range. I left a voice message." She paused. "It might take awhile for him to get back to me."

Sam gave her cell and home numbers—didn't mention that the sheriff's department had already responded to one call from her today. She debated waiting for him but it could be hours. She didn't want to stand around in the pouring rain, staring at the grave but from this morning's instructions by Deputy Beau she figured she better not work indoors either. She tapped an impatient toe as heavy raindrops saturated the freshly cut lawn. It seemed to be tapering off. She dashed for the front door, gathered her tools and locked the newly installed lock.

The strange events of the day were wearing her down; she thought of her friend Zoe, who operated a homey B&B

with her husband Darryl. The rain had slowed to a drizzle and blue sky began to show in the west. This was usually how New Mexico rainstorms went. Sam pushed her mower up into the utility trailer, backed the little rig around and headed into town, envisioning a cup of tea and some good conversation to smooth over the afternoon.

She'd just reached the intersection of Highway 64, when her cell rang.

"Samantha Sweet? This is Beau Cardwell. Two bodies in one day? I have to say, that might be some kind of record."

She couldn't tell if he was irritated or joking so she quickly explained about finding the grave and how she'd quit mowing the minute she found it. "Is it legal to bury someone on private property?"

"With a permit, usually it's fine," he said. "But since the place was abandoned, it might be smart for me to check it out. Don't touch anything until I can get some answers."

She told him about her plans for Zoe's, clicked off the call and drove on. The Chartrain's B&B was right in the middle of Taos, a hundred-year-old house sitting on a winding lane amid picturesque adobe neighbors. Maneuvering Sam's truck and trailer in there would be iffy, so she drove to her own house on Elmwood Lane, two blocks away. A narrow drive led to the back of the property, where she had a good, wide turnaround spot. She parked there and walked over to the B&B. The rain shower, which had drenched the county west of the Rio Grande, apparently hadn't touched this part of town at all.

Zoe was out front, knee deep in a bed of wildflowers, rose bushes and zinnias. Hollyhocks in full pink and burgundy bloom towered behind her and a graceful weeping willow draped its slim branches over a pond on the northwest corner of the lot. Zoe wiped a wisp of stray hair out of her eyes and tucked it behind her ear.

"Hey," she greeted in her soft voice. Wearing a gauzy skirt and tank top, with leather sandals on not-quite-clean feet, she looked every bit the child of the commune in which she'd been raised. Her parents were some of the true free-love hippies of the '60s and Zoe never gave up her roots. It wasn't until she met Darryl ten years ago, that she settled into married life at thirty. The B&B came about as a result of their love of people and the fact that Darryl had inherited the six-bedroom house when his father passed away. Sam had the feeling that Zoe would rather simply tend the huge organic garden out back, but rave reviews on both the accommodations and their bountiful table kept her interested in the business.

"What's going on?" Zoe said, dusting soil from her hands. She gave Sam an intent look and her pale brows pulled together. "Something's happened, Sam. You look upset."

"Do I?"

"Yes, you do." She picked up a watering can and tipped it to rinse her left hand, switched and rinsed the right, while Sam gave a quick recap of both of the day's strange events.

"The sheriff will check on the grave, but they don't want me out there right now. I was thinking . . ."

". . . about a cup of tea."

"Chai, if you have it."

Zoe kicked a bunch of clippings into a little pile and then led the way around the side of the low adobe, to the kitchen door. Just inside, she kicked off the Birkenstocks, wiped her bare feet on the mat, and headed toward the kitchen sink, giving her hands a good scrubbing before reaching for the cookie jar.

"Here—I still have a couple of your brownies that the guests didn't get."

Sam stepped up to the sink and washed off the dust, rust and weird feeling that she seemed to have picked up during her morning labors. Zoe's kitchen was a cheerful place, painted in soft terra cotta with lots of bright Mexican tile, large copper pots hanging from ceiling hooks, and a round table with fuschia and yellow placemats and cloth napkins. It always smelled of Mexican vanilla. Darryl remodeled it about two years ago, bringing in the latest professional appliances and knocking out a divider wall so there was plenty of room around the island counter for guests to have their first cup of coffee as the muffins were coming out of the oven. They loved that homey atmosphere.

Zoe brought chai mix out of the pantry and put the kettle on to boil.

"It's the first time I've found anything like . . . death . . . at my properties, and now twice in one day."

"You don't find it kind of spooky going out to those houses and sneaking in?" She pulled a colorfully painted plate from the cabinet and put brownies on it. "I mean, there has to be some strange energy in those abandoned places." She set the plate on the counter near the barstools.

"So far, in the months I've been doing this, it's been pretty tame," Sam said. "Usually just a lot of junk that has to be hauled off before the authorities can consider holding an auction. I had one place where the trash filled a whole roll-off Dumpster. Once the clutter is out, most places clean up pretty well." She didn't mention the time she'd come across the earmarks of a meth lab. That one had been in the middle of town and local police came right in and handled it. Since it was only her second property after taking the job, Delbert Crow had taken over and she'd been out of the picture quickly.

The kettle whistled and Zoe poured, stirring in the chai. She joined Sam at the counter and Sam was well into her second brownie when her phone rang.

She swallowed a hunk of the brownie and saw the caller was Deputy Cardwell.

"Sam? Are you still at that property where you found the grave?"

"No. I left after the rain shower."

"Things are pretty well stacked up this afternoon and I can't get there until tomorrow. But I'd like to have you meet us there—say eight in the morning?"

Sam wasn't eager to visit the grave again. There had been such an eerie feeling around it. But she had to finish cleaning the house and tending the yard, and it would be easier to approach it for the second time with the authorities there.

"If you get there first, don't touch anything," he said. "It's potentially a crime scene."

Chapter 4

Sam left Zoe's place with a brief sugar high but it quickly faded when she got home. Too much excitement. She briefly considered sitting in on the mystery book discussion at Mysterious Happenings that evening but it seemed like an effort. The peace and quiet of her own home, enjoyed in solitude, were much more appealing.

As she got out of the truck she spotted Bertha Martinez's little wooden box on the back seat. Why had the woman insisted that Sam, a total stranger, was meant to have it? Maybe she was just a lonely old woman with no friends or family. The box might have been her only prized possession. Maybe she just wanted to hand it over to someone, rather than letting it get shucked off to the thrift shop. Her final words, though, hovered in Sam's head.

She set the box on her kitchen table and dumped her pack and keys beside it. A chunk of cheddar, an apple and a few plain saltines were going to suffice for dinner. The box pulled her attention as she nibbled at them.

In the late-afternoon light of her kitchen, Sam noticed details that had escaped her in the flurried moments at Bertha Martinez's house as she grabbed the box from the dresser, rushed to place it in the safety of the truck, and then dashed back inside to try to summon help for the dying woman.

The piece was made of wood, carved with deep criss-crossed grooves, like something thickly quilted. At each X where the lines crossed, a small cabochon stone was mounted, held in place by tiny metal prongs. Sam flipped on overhead track lights to get a better look. The stones appeared to be malachite, lapis and coral. The greens, blues and reds winked with unexpected brightness under the lights. A metal hasp with a simple twist mechanism held the lid closed.

It might have been an attractive piece but for the fact that it was crudely done. The cuts were uneven and the puffed areas not uniform in size or depth. Not childish, exactly, but not the work of a craftsman either. The finish was garish, the stain too yellow, the recesses too dark. Maybe she could take some polish to it.

She pushed her plate aside and sat down again with the box before her. It was heavy for its size, maybe eight inches by six and no more than four inches deep. She twisted the clasp and tried to raise the lid but it seemed stuck.

The knife she'd used to slice the cheese worked. Something old and sticky crackled and the lid creaked upward, hinged at the back.

A wisp of smoke rose out of it—a thin curl of red, green and blue. It dissipated so quickly that within three seconds Sam swore she must have imagined it.

But she didn't. The box suddenly felt warm to the touch and she set it down with a clatter.

It sat there on the woven placemat on the table. Staring at her.

She reached out a tentative finger and touched it. Cool again. Not a scrap of warmth there.

Was this what Bertha Martinez meant? Maybe it was made of some particular wood that warmed to a human touch.

Sam grasped the edges of the lid and rocked it closed and open again, twice more, feeling the old hinges loosen. The surface still felt cool to the touch. Pulling the box a little closer, she peered inside. Empty. The wood inside was plain, stained the same sour yellow as the outside, not finely sanded or varnished. She ran her index finger around the inner edges, feeling for any little clue—something carved, anything. The moment her finger completed the circuit of the fourth side, a jolt—nearly electrical—zapped up her arm, clear to the shoulder.

She fell out of her chair, hit with a wave of dizziness that nearly blinded her.

Chapter 5

Sam awoke in her bed, with no recollection of getting there. Bright sunlight came through the east-facing windows. She started—was she late to meet the sheriff's people at eight? She rolled toward her bedside clock and found that it was only six-thirty. Normally with that kind of time to spare she would roll over and let herself drift off again. But she felt curiously wide awake.

She sat up and took stock. She was fully dressed in yesterday's clothes. The last time that happened was twenty years ago after a bad encounter with several shots of tequila. She was not obsessive about routines, but she did at least brush her teeth, wash her face, and put on a nightshirt before falling into bed. Always.

Wandering into the living room she noticed that she'd

not locked her front deadbolt; two lamps were burning; and on the kitchen table sat that wooden box.

It has special powers. The box holds many truths.

Bertha Martinez's final words buzzed in her head.

Too weird. Sam shook off the feeling. She'd just been overtired, loaded with sugar from her stopover at Zoe's, and she had some kind of strange . . . episode. She didn't know what. She'd probably just dozed off at the kitchen table and then automatically wandered off to bed. That made the most sense.

A shower and fresh clothes were the answer. She bustled into the bathroom and rushed through her routine, feeling an eagerness to get on with the day. Normally a slow riser and groggy morning person, she knew this energy was proof positive that all was right with the world. Grooming consisted of finger-combing her shaggy, graying hair and touching on a little lip gloss. She donned a pair of jeans and one of her work shirts, ready to face the cleanup job at the county property once Beau Cardwell got whatever formalities out of the way.

She didn't want to waste any time. As it was, her arrival would probably coincide with the deputy's. She packed a little cooler with a peanut butter sandwich, two apples and a half-empty bag of corn chips, plus a granola bar that she was going to call breakfast. Two diet Cokes rounded out her stash of lunch and snack food to last the day.

By the time she pulled up in front of the property, still known to her as #23 County Road 4, a cruiser and another county vehicle were already there. Beau Cardwell stood at the open door of the cruiser in his crisp dark uniform and Stetson, speaking into the mike on his shoulder. Sam approached, pocketing the key to her truck. He made some kind of over-and-out remark to the microphone. When he turned, he sent a smile her way—impersonal at first but then it became a long, assessing look.

For the first time she noticed that he had incredible shoulders and Sam guessed him to be a bit younger than herself, probably in his late forties. Dark hair with sprinkles of gray and sideburns nearly white. Blue eyes, the color of deep ocean, distracted her as he pulled out a clipboard with some forms on it.

Stop it, she admonished herself, *you are* not *interested.* She tugged her shirttails down and turned her attention away from Beau.

Two men, both in uniform, were approaching. The one in charge was about her height, maybe five-five or –six, Hispanic, forty-ish, with a solid paunch. Cardwell quickly introduced him as Sheriff Orlando Padilla.

"There's no permit on record for that grave," Padilla said to Sam. "We also checked county death records for the past six months and cross referenced them with burial records. We don't have any death certificates without records of where burial took place. That's why we're treating this as a potential crime scene. We'll need to take a look inside the house."

"The grave is actually out at the back edge of the lawn," Sam said.

Cardwell sent her a wry grin. "Let's take a look out there first, then you can unlock the house." He gestured toward the backyard. "Show us what you found."

She led the way, noticing how she'd cut the grass yesterday. Nice clean rows near the house, one trail toward the back, an abrupt stop. The mound of dirt was still mainly surrounded by tall grass but she stood aside and pointed toward it. While the three men poked around in the tall grass Sam went back and unlocked the front door, crossed through the living room and kitchen and came out the back.

Padilla stood with hands on hips, glanced at the ground, looked at Beau. Sam stood by, wishing she could just get on with her job.

"Do you know when Anderson vacated the place?" It took Sam a second to realize Beau was talking to her.

"I think our records indicated that the owner left sometime in March or April."

Padilla turned to him. "Well, no permit, we have to dig." He stared at the younger deputy, a stout kid in his twenties, who grimaced and headed for his patrol car. He came back a minute later with a shovel. Sam got the feeling the pudgy young guy would rather that the more physically fit Beau do the digging but he didn't say anything.

"Start on this," Padilla told him. "Cardwell, you take a look in the house. I have to get back to town."

Beau touched Sam's elbow in a gentlemanly way. She looked up at him, but he'd turned back to be sure the other deputy was shoveling. She headed toward the house and let him in the back door.

It led directly into the kitchen. People who skipped out didn't seem to feel the need to wash dishes or clean up. A trash can in one corner overflowed, primarily with fast food wrappers, pizza boxes and paper plates. All the real dishes were stacked in the sink and on counters. Sam didn't even want to guess at the guck that had dried onto them.

She felt a little embarrassed by the mess, as if she'd invited a guest into her own home and they'd found it in this condition. But Beau didn't seem to care. He gave the kitchen a glance, ignoring the trash and the table, which she'd just noticed was covered in beer cans with a half eaten pizza dried to a crisp in its box. He'd walked into the living room.

Almost on auto pilot, Sam went to the sink and tested to see if there was hot water. After a minute the cold stream became warm, then hot, then steamy. She found a nearly empty bottle of dish detergent under the sink and squirted it liberally over the haphazard stack. Stoppering the basin, she let the whole thing fill with hot water.

"Sam?" The deputy's voice came from another room. "You're not moving anything, are you?"

Oh shit. In her haste to make the place presentable, she'd forgotten that the whole house might be considered part of the crime scene.

He strode in from the other room. "Don't tell me you're washing away our evidence. Please don't tell me that."

She'd turned off the faucet but the sudsy basin gave her away. "Deputy, I . . . should I let the water out?"

He stared down at her from his six and a half feet, eyes dark beneath the Stetson. "No, it's okay."

She felt like a complete idiot. Hadn't she watched enough episodes of *CSI* to know that you didn't touch a thing at a crime scene?

He glanced out the back window, noticing that the younger deputy had quit digging. He opened the back door. "Relax. And just call me Beau." He seemed about to say something more but turned away instead.

She watched him walk to the back of the property. Suppressing the urge to bag the trash, she jammed her hands into her pockets and stepped out to the back porch. She could see that the deputies had found something. The shovel stuck up from the ground and the young guy was squatting at the edge of the hole, tugging at something. Beau, too, hunkered down examining the object. Curiosity piqued her interest but she wasn't sure she wanted to know the details, close up. After a minute or two Beau stood and spoke into his shoulder mike. He brushed dirt off his hands and walked back toward the house.

From the porch step Sam was exactly eye level with him as he stopped to speak.

"There's a body, all right," he said. "It's wrapped in blankets, not exactly a funeral director's style. We're going to need to exhume and identify it."

Exhume, as in dig up and bring out into the open. Sam *really* didn't want to know too much about that.

"It would take me probably another week to get a team of crime lab folks out here from Santa Fe, and this isn't exactly a fresh scene. It's just that Padilla and myself will be the only qualified ones in the office the rest of the week—"

"Could I help in some way? Is that what you're trying to say?"

"Well, yeah." He actually scuffed the toe of his boot in the dirt. "It would just be to go through things in the house and try to get more information about the owner."

She shrugged. "It's what I do." As long as she didn't have to get a good up-close look at a decomposing body, she was happy with any other little task. Plus, the sooner this whole thing was resolved, the sooner she'd finish her real job here and be able to submit her invoice. And that meant a check. And that meant groceries.

Damn Kelly, Sam thought. *It's an awful way to feel about my own daughter, but cleaning out my checking account was a shitty thing.*

She suppressed that line of thought and stepped back into the messy kitchen.

"What kind of information do you want me to look for?" she asked. "Anderson's relatives, that kind of thing?"

He grinned at her. "You're getting the idea. You'll make a great assistant deputy."

"Isn't a deputy already an assistant?"

"Yeah, but we're kind of winging it here. Unless you want to go out there and help pull the body out of the grave, you'll have to be content without an official swearing in." Was he *flirting*?

"Trust me, I'm very content not to be sworn in. Just tell me what I have to do to get on with cleaning this place up."

"Okay. We need papers, bills, checks—anything that might let us know more about Anderson. How long ago since anyone last heard from him. That sort of thing."

"There's a desk in a corner of the living room. I can start with that." He handed her a pair of surgical gloves and she cut through the kitchen, refusing to look at the heaping trashcan and piles of food-encrusted dishes. Beau followed, poking at the bathroom door, using a ballpoint pen to pull drawers open, scanning the rooms quickly to get a general feel for the layout.

"He must have had someone else living here," Sam observed. "Both bedrooms look lived in. I mean, one guy living here alone—even a husband and wife—there's going to be one bedroom used and the other as a spare, right?"

"Good observation, assistant." He *was* flirting! Sam noticed how there was the tiniest gap near one of his incisors; he had a habit of smiling slightly wider on that side of his mouth. It had the effect of making him human, dimming slightly the otherwise near perfect looks. *Stop thinking about that!*

"Both beds are rumpled, there are clothes in both closets," he said, stepping back into the hallway. "I'll canvass a few of the neighbors later. The medical investigator should be getting here soon."

Like a prophecy coming true, they heard a vehicle pull up to the house. Beau went out the front door while Sam turned back to her work. Through the open drapes at the back bedroom window she could see him showing a man in a suit out to the gravesite, the same guy who'd been at Bertha Martinez's yesterday. The men were standing over a bundle of cloth, the blankets Beau had mentioned. The bundle hardly looked large enough to contain a person, she thought with a pang.

She pulled open the first of the desk drawers. So, Mr. Riley Anderson, who were you? Are you the sad little heap out there in the yard now, or did you put someone else there?

Chapter 6

Beau and the younger deputy loaded the blanketed bundle into the back of the OMI vehicle to be taken to Albuquerque for autopsy, and saw the man off before coming back into the house. They worked with Sam for a couple of hours side by side, until the men pretty well decided that they weren't going to find blood stains, bullet holes or signs of violent death. The goal now was to identify the body, so Beau took fingerprints from several surfaces. Two radio calls had come in while they worked and they were beginning to feel the squeeze to attend to other cases. Sam agreed to box up whatever bills or personal papers she came across and turn them over. Otherwise, she was free to clean the place to her heart's content.

She filled four garbage bags in the kitchen, threw them into her truck. Scrubbed the appliances, put away dishes, sanitized countertops and floors. In the other rooms, she gathered books and trinkets and boxed them for her favorite thrift shop. There was a book on plants that she thought Zoe would like, and a couple of mysteries that Ivan might be able to sell in his shop. The rules allowed her to distribute the household furnishings in the way she saw fit, so she tried to make the best use of everything. Furniture stayed with the house, those pieces in decent condition. Sometimes they weren't, and the trashed-out things would be hauled to the dump.

She spent some time at the desk in the living room, gathering statements from the local bank, unpaid utility bills with progressively harsh warnings and scraps of anything that might provide the sheriff with clues about Anderson's life. The only thing remotely menacing was a letter from an attorney. Dated nearly a year earlier, it addressed a claim by an adjoining property owner that Anderson's fence was two feet over the boundary. The neighbor, Leonard Trujillo, was insisting that Anderson move the fence or pay him for the 'stolen' land. Sam's guess was that if Anderson couldn't pay his own mortgage, he sure couldn't pay a neighbor the ridiculous amount the letter alleged that he owed for a tiny strip of land. She crammed all the papers into a shoebox, setting the attorney's letter on top where the sheriff's people would easily see it. Finally, she closed the drawers and wiped her dusty hands on her jeans.

Grabbing a duster Sam hit the door jambs and corners, swiping away the cobwebs that seemingly appeared overnight in this part of the country. She noticed quite a number of nails in the walls; there had once been a lot of pictures hung, and by the spacing she guessed that they were larger pieces of art, not just family photos. But they were gone now.

With the living, dining, kitchen and bathroom in good

shape, she tackled the two bedrooms, starting with the smaller. Beau and the deputy had taken several items—clothes and bedding—that might provide DNA for matching with the body in the grave. Sam bagged the rest of the clothing for the trip to the thrift shop. Male, size medium, whose taste ran to rugby shirts and chinos. The bed in this room consisted of a mattress on the floor and it was lumpy looking and stained so it went out to her truck, added to the load for the dump.

The larger, master bedroom seemed to be where the law enforcement guys had concentrated so there wasn't much left. They took all the bedding, the contents of the bedside stand, and some clothing from closet and dresser. Sam began going through the pockets of every remaining garment, as she'd promised Beau she would do, before tossing the item into the charity bag.

In the pocket of a pair of brown slacks, she came across a narrow slip of yellow paper, like a store receipt. Except it was written as a promissory note, with Anderson agreeing to pay someone named Harry Woodruff, the sum of four hundred dollars for "merchandise received." That was all. No name of the store, no explanation of the purchase. Just someone who gave Anderson credit. It was dated two years ago, so the odds were that the debt had been paid or the man had forgotten about it, but Sam saved the slip for the sheriff's investigators anyway.

Garments continued to fill the bag. All of the clothing was old, as its owner must have been. From the styles of the shirts, pants and shoes, he was a slight man who was probably in his seventies or so. Most everything was well worn, and many of the pieces had paint stains on them. When she reached the far corner of the closet shelf she discovered a box with brushes and paints which explained the condition of his things.

Sam immediately thought of her friend, Rupert Penrick, who probably had friends who might like the supplies. She set the box aside for him.

With the closet clear, she brought in the vacuum cleaner and started to work with the crevice tool. The far reaches were coated in dust balls and cobwebs and she quickly did away with them. Closets always sell a house, so she wanted this one to look as big and unencumbered as possible. She switched on the light and opened the bedroom drapes to see the space better. And then she noticed something strange.

The far wall of the closet was painted very crudely, almost as if someone had taken white shoe polish to it. They were clearly trying to cover up something else, because a design of some kind showed through in a few places. She grabbed a bottle of spray cleaner and decided to check it out.

As she rubbed at one corner of the area, the cheap white over-coat came away, revealing a scene underneath. The more she worked, the larger the hidden painting became. It was a mural, a rural scene done in an impressionistic style. Odd. What a strange place for a painted mural. She worked at it a little more until the entire scene was revealed. And in the lower corner was a signature. Pierre Cantone.

Her pulse quickened. *The* Pierre Cantone? No art expert, what little Sam knew had rubbed off from time spent around Rupert, but she knew the name Pierre Cantone. It was like saying have you heard of Renoir or Picasso. Everyone had heard of Cantone. What on earth was Riley Anderson up to? Copying a famous artist's work, maybe for practice? Or . . . an even more astounding thought . . . could it be possible that the famous artist had once stayed at this house? Before Anderson bought it? Maybe the old man had unknowingly painted over a real masterpiece.

She pulled her cell phone from her pocket and dialed Rupert's number.

"What are you doing?" she asked the second she heard his voice.

"I'm writing, Sam. It's what I do. Every day. I'm two hundred pages into *Love's Velvet Hammer* and you wouldn't have caught me except that I just paused for a quick lunch break." Rupert was an aging writer, former Little Theatre actor, and art aficionado who secretly wrote romance novels under the name of Victoria DeVane. He made a fantastic amount of money, as Victoria was always at the top of the bestseller lists, but only the closest of friends knew his true identity because even his editor says that men can't write romances.

"Good," Sam said. "I've got something here that you have to see."

"Where? Your house?"

"No, sorry. I'm at one of my break-ins. I may have just found an original Pierre Cantone."

"Ohmygod! No way!"

"I'm pretty sure. Well, okay, I'm not at all sure. I don't know this stuff, but there's a mural on one wall, about two feet by three feet big, his style, and his signature."

"Girl—" He breathed the word more than he said it.

"If you want to come out here . . ."

Very little would get Rupert to vary his writing schedule, but art was one thing and a find of this type would definitely do it. Sam gave him directions and he said he'd be there in ten minutes. That worried her a little, since the place was at least twenty minutes from town. But Rupert was known for driving his Mini-Cooper like a Formula-1 racer.

She began to have pangs the minute she hung up. She really should have told Beau Cardwell about this first. She dialed his direct number from the card he'd left with her and quickly explained the find.

"It's painted right on the wall?" he said.

She confirmed.

"Well, then I guess it's not going anywhere very soon. You got a camera with you?"

"Out in the truck." She carried one for the occasional property where she might need to document something really unusual for her supervisor. "I'll get some pictures."

"Good. And don't paint over it or anything. I may need to come back out there at some point and take a look."

Paint over it? Like that would happen. She would, however, be lucky if Rupert didn't bring a saw with him and want to take out the wall.

"Any word yet on the identity of the body in the grave?" she asked.

He chuckled. "Sam, it's only been three hours since I was there."

Really? She glanced at her watch. Holy cow. She'd blazed her way through the house in record time. The kitchen alone would have normally taken longer than that. And she didn't even feel tired.

True to his word, Rupert showed up minutes later. They sat in front of the closet door, staring at the mural. He'd run his hands lovingly over the paint, verifying that it wasn't just some kind of decal or trick of decoupage or something. No, it truly was an original, painted right there. But was it a Cantone?

"A skillful artist who loves Cantone's style could have

copied it, couldn't he?" Sam asked, pointing out the box of paints and brushes she'd found. "Maybe Mr. Anderson just wanted to experiment—test his own talent?"

"An expert would have to authenticate it, of course," Rupert said. "But the strange thing is that this scene is unknown. What would the other artist have copied from?"

"So, he made it up? Copied Cantone's style and signature?"

He made a little grimacing move with his mouth. "Maybe. But why put it here? Someone wants to copy a famous artist they're usually trying to make some money. And someone *this* good, sweetie, I can tell you. This guy could be making good money even if he admitted his work was a fake. Passing it off as real—he'd have a chance of pulling it off, selling to some rich dude who didn't bother to verify, for a couple hundred thou."

Whoa. Sam had no idea Cantone's work was worth that.

She showed Rupert the digital photos she'd taken and he shot a couple more, zooming in on the signature and a few details.

"I'll get these to an appraiser I know in Santa Fe," he said. "If he thinks there's a chance this is real, he'll probably want to come out and see it."

Sam cautioned him about trying to remove the painting, that the sheriff still considered the property a crime scene, which led to a whole explanation about finding the grave in the backyard.

After Rupert left she finished tidying up the bedroom and looked around. She'd never finished a cleanup job this quickly. A little more work out in the yard, which at this rate she could easily finish this afternoon, and the place would be ready to list for sale. Sam debated. She really needed the money, and to get paid she'd have to submit her report and allow access to the house by others. On the other hand, it would kill her to let someone come in here and paint over a potentially valuable work of art. The first Realtor in the door would probably want to do that. For now, she would hold off awhile.

The county landfill was on her way home so Sam stopped there and dumped off the bags of trash and the stained old mattress. Next stop was at the thrift shop on Paseo del Pueblo Norte, where she left the clothing she'd collected and a couple boxes of stuff that might have some value to them—books, a damaged lamp that might be repaired, some kitchen utensils. She wanted to get the book on plants to Zoe so, after she'd parked her truck and trailer at home, she walked over to the B&B.

Zoe was pouring herself a glass of wine when Sam walked into her kitchen and she accepted one too. Exclaiming over the book Zoe carried it with her as they went out to the shady patio to relax.

"You finished an entire property in one day?" she asked, groaning as she sank into a wicker chair. "I barely got my flower beds weeded and I'm aching all over."

Sam murmured something about being a little bundle of energy today.

"Hey, this is a great book," Zoe said, flipping through the pages. "Interesting . . . here's a whole section on deadly stuff."

"Ha—you'll be known as the queen of mushrooms."

Sam's cell phone vibrated in her pocket just then, making

her jump. Rupert.

"Hey, girl. I heard from that appraiser? He wants to come out and see the mural. Tomorrow?"

"That was fast."

"Beauty of email," he said. "So, you think it will be okay for us to come up?"

"Just to take a look, sure. I can't let you take it away until the sheriff's department gives the okay, though."

"Okay then. I'll send a positive vibe out to the universe that this is the real thing and that we get to bring it back."

She thought about that as he hung up. If it truly was a valuable painting, the proceeds belonged to the owner's estate. If Anderson turned out to be the dead guy, by rights the lien holder on the property could claim up to the value of their unpaid balance against it. Seemed a shame but she really should report the find to Delbert Crow. That prospect deflated her. She stuck the phone back in her pocket and took a big swig of her wine.

Zoe's husband Darryl came out the back door, carrying a bottled beer. "Hey, I wondered where you were. Hey, Sam."

"Just taking a break. My dogs were killing me," Zoe said, wiggling her bare toes. She'd kicked off her sandals and put her feet up on a small wicker stool.

"Here," he said, "let me give them a little TLC." He set his beer on the side table and rubbed his hands together briskly before reaching for one of her feet. Darryl is a teddy bear of a guy, burly, with gray hair that hangs below his shoulders and a full white beard. He's a plumbing contractor and Sam had seen him at construction sites, hollering at his crew to hurry it up. Then he came home and absolutely doted on Zoe, like now, rubbing her feet when she was tired or volunteering to make dinner at the end of a long day. He was a prize.

Zoe leaned back in the chair and let him start a massage on her toes.

"I'll take the other one," Sam said. "We'll just pamper you a little."

She set her glass down and knelt near the footstool. When Sam touched Zoe's bare foot she jerked it back.

"Sorry. Cold hands?"

"No," she said. "Go ahead. It just startled me."

This time she reacted to the touch but didn't pull away. Sam felt warmth flow from her hands to her friend's foot.

Zoe sat up straight. "What *is* that?"

"I don't know." She was momentarily speechless. Some energizing force had gone down her arms, out her fingertips, and into Zoe's foot. Without thinking, she drew both hands from the back of Zoe's heel, along the sides of her foot, out the length of her toes. As she let go of the foot, Zoe let out a pent-up breath. Darryl stopped and stared at her.

Sam stood up quickly and shook out her hands. "That was weird."

"Very weird." Zoe stood on the tile patio, shifting her weight from one foot to the other.

"My left foot feels tingly and not at all achy. The right one is about the same as it was before. Sorry, honey. No offense to your massage skills." She took a few steps that turned into a little jig. "I cannot believe how much better it feels. The aches and pains are completely gone."

Whoa. Did this go along with the fact that Sam had just cleaned a whole house and yard, with energy to spare?

Darryl shook his head. "I can't believe this."

Zoe was exuberant. "Do the other one, Sam. Start at my

knee and do my leg as well."

She had no idea what to think but followed her friend's instruction. One stroke from knee to toes and Zoe was practically dancing. She grabbed Sam in a big hug. But Sam noticed that Darryl looked at her differently, suspiciously.

"I wouldn't go around advertising this," he said.

Somehow, she knew he was right.

Chapter 7

Sam called Beau Cardwell when she got home, explained Rupert's interest in the mural and suggested that he would probably want to get there before the art appraiser arrived. Then she phoned Delbert Crow, interrupting his dinner, and told him in vague terms that she'd found an item that was physically attached to the house that should be removed before the home was listed for sale. He didn't seem to mind that they cut a hole in the wall, as long as Sam patched it with fresh wallboard; he was more disgruntled at her recommendation that the entire interior be repainted. Probably ninety-percent of the reclaimed homes warranted a fresh coat of paint before resale but Crow said to let it go; a buyer at a foreclosure sale would expect to repaint the place himself. Fine.

Sam gathered tools and a spare piece of drywall that she knew she'd stashed out in the garage somewhere. Luckily she'd helped her dad with enough construction projects when she was a kid that she knew what to do. This wouldn't be that big a repair.

Everything went into the truck. She microwaved a frozen dinner and ate it in front of the TV. She studiously avoided handling the wooden box that still sat on her kitchen table, or thinking too much about the strange experience at Zoe's house that afternoon.

By eight the next morning Sam was on the familiar-feeling route to the Anderson place. Beau was waiting in the driveway and she remembered that she had not left a key or lockbox yet.

"Place is looking good," he commented as they walked through the living room.

"The painting is back here." She showed him the small mural hidden in the closet.

"Hold this tape measure up for reference," he said, pulling out a camera. He snapped a few shots. "I guess that's all we would need. Can't think of any way this is going to change our investigation. We don't even know yet if there's anything suspicious about this death."

Sam handed back the tape and his fingers touched hers. The closet felt suddenly intimate, with the two of them crowded in there. Beau leaned toward her, ever so slightly, as if he wanted to say something. Sam bumped into the wall behind her.

Heavy footfalls on the porch and a knock at the door interrupted.

Beau sent her a searching look, which she tried to ignore.

"Hellloooo . . . " Rupert's voice echoed through the house.

She slipped past Beau and peered out the bedroom door. "In here," she called.

Rupert tended to float into a room, his trademark purple scarves and full-sleeved tunic shirts billowing, the gestures and number of scarves increasing in correlation to the size of his audience. Considering that he was nearly six feet tall and weighed over two hundred pounds, he was pretty hard to miss in a crowd. He preceded the appraiser who introduced himself as Esteban, a thin, dark-haired man in a business suit, that Sam guessed to be in his mid-twenties.

She introduced Beau to the other two but it was apparent that Rupert couldn't wait to show off the mural, and Beau seemed eager to get on the road. While the two art hounds crowded in near the painting, she saw Beau out to the front porch.

He got to the bottom step and turned. "I started to ask if you would have dinner with me. Tomorrow night?"

Sam almost blurted out, *why?*, but stopped herself at the last second. Guys like Beau Cardwell—tall, calendar material—did not date women like Samantha Sweet— average, chunky, with strands of gray in their hair. It just did not happen.

"A date?" she asked. It had been *way* too many years.

"Why not? You're a beautiful lady." He actually sounded sincere.

"Beautiful? You've only seen me in jeans that are coated in dust," she countered. "Besides, I don't really *date* much."

"Okay, we'll call it dinner for two friends who want to get to know each other better." This time, he really sounded sincere.

She debated.

To question why a guy wants to share a meal with you isn't polite. And if there's one thing she'd learned growing up in west Texas, it's that a lady is always polite. She accepted.

She watched him climb into the department SUV and drive away. Well. This would be interesting.

Excited voices inside the house caught her attention. She walked into the living room where Rupert met her in a flurry.

"Sam—" He was nearly breathless. "Esteban is very encouraged."

"He thinks it's real?"

The appraiser stepped out of the bedroom. "Is early to say." He had some kind of Spanish/French euro-accent, which seemed completely affected. "I must run tests."

Rupert was practically twitching with anticipation, while Esteban played it cool, ruffling the pages of a magazine that Sam had left lying on the coffee table.

She shrugged. "My supervisor said that it was okay to remove it."

Rupert nearly drooled.

"I'll need to get a receipt. It belongs to the estate of the home owner."

Esteban reached into an inner pocket in his jacket and pulled out a small book. He might look like a cool customer but he'd come prepared. While he filled out a receipt and signed it, Sam went out to her truck and brought in the tools.

Neither of the men looked eager to get drywall dust on their clothes so Sam drilled four corner holes, inserted the wallboard saw and started taking out a section about twelve inches larger all around than the actual painting. They wrapped their treasure in a blanket that Esteban had conveniently remembered to bring and drove away in Rupert's Mini Cooper, both looking happy as clams.

Sam watched the plume of dust settle on the road and walked back to her truck to get the sheet of drywall she'd brought along to repair the gaping hole in the wall. About the time she'd measured the hole, brought the saw back outside, and cut a replacement piece she realized that she had company. A woman wearing pink capris and a loose, floral-patterned T-shirt was coming up the drive. Sam guessed her to be in her seventies, with peach-tinted hair almost covered by a pink floppy hat.

"I saw your truck here yesterday, too," the lady said by way of greeting.

Sam gave the quick explanation of her role as caretaker. She still found it amazing how often she spent days at a place, carted away half the furniture and no one even raised an eyebrow.

The woman stuck out her hand. "Betty McDonald. My husband and I live at the next place over." She waved vaguely toward the west. Sam spotted another simple wood frame house about a hundred yards away. "Been here since before Riley bought his place five years ago. Way before his *friend* moved in, the young one." Her eyebrows formed a pair of golden arches.

"Oh, were you *friends* with Mr. Anderson too?" Sam knew what she was hinting at when she said *friend*, and couldn't resist the little dig back at her.

Betty ignored it. "The sheriff's deputy came around yesterday, asking me about them. I told him what little I knew. Riley Anderson wasn't all that neighborly. In fact, Leonard Trujillo had to get nasty with him. See that fence over there?" She pointed to the property on the opposite side of Anderson's place from her own. "Riley put that up and it was on Leonard's land. Leonard threatened to sue him."

Sam didn't mention that she already knew this little tidbit.

"Most of the other neighbors wouldn't even talk to him, but I'd stop in now and then, just to check on him. I'd see him puttering around the yard. He seemed to like working in the flower beds. But after the other one moved in, Riley didn't show his face much."

Sam recalled the haphazard mess in the second bedroom, clothes strewn about, the unmade mattress on the floor. He might have been a slob but there was no evidence that Betty's sly insinuation was true. "How long did the other guy live here?"

Betty rolled her eyes upward, remembering. "I'd say he moved in around the beginning of the spring. Four or five months maybe? No. You know when it was? St. Patrick's Day. March 17. I remember because I was heading into town to meet some other Irish friends for a traditional dinner. Corned beef—um, I love that stuff. That's when the strange blue car showed up."

Of course. The perfect busybody neighbor who watched everyone's comings and goings.

Betty went on. "I only saw Riley a few times after that. He didn't look so good. I stopped in once with some muffins I'd baked and he said he'd been sick a lot. I gave him the name of my doctor in town but he wouldn't go, told me he didn't believe in doctors. After that, I would see the blue car come and go, not very often though. They mostly stayed around the house. Then Bill and I went on vacation the first week of June. When we came back, Riley's old pickup and the other guy's car were both gone. Place looked empty. Never saw either one of them again."

When Betty started repeating things, Sam knew she was out of information so she started rummaging through her tool box, hinting that she still had work to do.

"Well, I need to get on with my walk," Betty said. "Can't be standing around here gabbing all day."

As if it were Sam's fault. Strange woman, she thought, as Betty walked back to the road and headed west.

Sam carried her rectangle of drywall back into the front bedroom and set it down, went back for the tape and joint compound. The studs behind the cut-out section might need some additional bracing. She tugged at the edges of the hole to see how sturdy it was. And then she noticed something odd.

Her sawing job had caused some of the old tape to split and a section of the old wall board now swung outward, as if a mini door had once been built into the wall. She pulled at it and a section about two feet tall came toward her. She reached for the flashlight they'd used earlier to look closely at the painting and shone it into the space behind the wall.

A couple of items seemed to be jammed in there. She reached in. Out came a leather-bound book, about fourteen inches tall and less than an inch thick. Along with it was a small pencil box made of wood. She wiped them against the carpet to take away some of the dust. The box was filled with art pencils, many of which were honed to fine points; obviously they'd been sharpened and resharpened many times. She ruffled the pages of the book. They were filled with sketches—a few human forms, but mostly botanical and architectural. There were European cathedrals, castles on hillsides, and even the soft adobe shapes of the Taos Pueblo. Then came pages and pages of plants—flowers and trees, mainly. She turned to the front of the book. Neatly lettered on the flyleaf were the words: Property of Pierre Cantone.

Her heart did a little flutter.

The world famous artist had held this book, had made these sketches.

Sam backed out of the closet and sat heavily on the edge of the bed. My god, she thought.

Cantone must have visited or lived in this house at some point. But why would he leave his sketchbook behind? And who had painted over the mural?

Chapter 8

Sam locked the house and took the sketchbook with her, wishing she knew more about the life of the artist, Pierre Cantone.

However, more pressing duties awaited. A quick call to Beau Cardwell got her the go-ahead to go back to Bertha Martinez's place and finish the cleanup there. His investigators were unable to locate any next-of-kin for the old woman, he said. It took Sam about twenty minutes to get past the crush of tourists meandering around the plaza. Taos's little town center really was pretty in the summer and autumn months, with lots of shady trees and hanging pots of bright flowers accenting adobe walls and freshly painted blue doors.

Too bad Sam couldn't say the same for Bertha's home. At one time the yard must have been nice, with a large cottonwood behind the house and a pair of matching blue spruce on either side of the front door, set off by beds of colorful flowers. But the old woman's declining health meant less time spent outdoors. Sam didn't have the time or the budget to replant and tend the place back to its former state, but at least she could trim and haul away last season's brown stalks and get rid of weeds that now sprouted in the driveway. She filled seven trash bags, and that was before she'd even unlocked the door.

Stale air rushed past her as she entered. Thank goodness she'd been able to get the authorities out here right when Bertha died. She couldn't even imagine what the place would be like, days later, if her body were still in here in the heat. She pushed that thought out of her head.

Bertha certainly had not been a housekeeper. But then, who is when they are old and ill? Sam started at the front door and worked her way toward the back. The living and dining areas were basically just messy. Books, magazines and papers everywhere. She grabbed a box from her truck and stacked the books inside—mostly non-fiction, they would be great items for the thrift shop. Newspapers and junk mail went into trash bags along with the dusty old candles and bundled herbs; she put a few envelopes containing utility bills into a stack to be turned over to Delbert Crow. A dust cloth and vacuum cleaner, some straightening of the furniture, and these rooms were in good shape. The kitchen and bath were a little more intensive, but the bagging and scrubbing went routinely. She knew that she was stalling about going into Bertha's bedroom but couldn't avoid it forever. Finally, she strode in there and whipped open the dark, cumbersome drapes and opened the windows to the warm September day.

Everything was just as she'd seen it on her previous trip, minus the dying woman in the bed. Beau said that the authorities had removed everything they wanted, so Sam approached the room with an exterminator's vengeance. None of the clothing was in decent shape for resale; the old woman probably hadn't bought a new item in twenty-five years. Into bags it went; the local quilting group might salvage some of the cloth that wasn't threadbare.

The medicine bottles weren't the kind from the pharmacy. A tentative sniff into one of them suggested herbal remedies, probably homemade. She wondered if Zoe might know anything about them. The idea of actually dipping in and taking any of the smelly concoctions gave her the creeps. But she put the few colored bottles into a small box to take with her.

By four o'clock she had to admit that she was dragging, wishing for another shot of yesterday's limitless energy. No lunch, a pickup truck full of bagged and boxed junk—that probably accounted for it. Other than a quick peek, she hadn't done anything with the second bedroom yet. Heavy drapes covered the room's single window so she had little sense of what awaited in there. And she really wanted to finish the place today so she could submit her billing and get on with other things.

She scrounged two granola bars from the glove box in her truck and consumed them with water in one of the freshly washed glasses in the kitchen. It helped some but, truthfully, she began to fantasize about the drive-through at Kentucky Fried Chicken on her way home. The image gave her enough umph to face the unopened second bedroom so she marched in there and flipped the light switch.

The overhead fixture held a red bulb, which gave the room the odd glow of a darkroom and she knew that wasn't going to be good enough to clean by. The heavy drapes were stuck in place with duct tape and it took her a couple of minutes to rip it away and pull them aside. Heavy clouds were again building outside and she heard a very distant rumble. Ominous. But nothing compared to the sight when she turned around.

There in the middle of the dark wood floor was a pentagram, laid out in white stones. Black candles, bundled herbs, a lot of animal symbols painted in white on red walls. Sam thought of the rumors of Bertha Martinez's involvement in witchcraft. Whoa—it looked like they were true.

Goosebumps tickled her scalp and she edged toward the open doorway. Her foot hit something and she spun around. A snake.

She shrieked and dashed for the door. Something clattered and she stared again at the reptile. It wasn't alive. The snake was a taxidermied one, posed in a wavy curl, as if he were slithering along the desert sand, except that his head was raised a few inches off the floor, teeth showing and tongue darting out. She stared at it, hugging the doorjamb, heart beating a thousand beats a second. She blew out a pent-up breath and realized some of the noise was coming from thunder, much closer now.

A flash of lightning lit every window, putting her in the middle of a strobe-filled maze of rooms. Her heart rate ratcheted up again. This can't be healthy, she told herself. She dashed for the front door and straight out to her truck, soaked by the downpour in the few seconds it took. She reached for the ignition before remembering that she'd left her keys on a table in the living room. She would have to go back in there.

Okay, Sam, calm down. She breathed slowly. *What's scaring you about this place anyway?* Well . . . symbols and witchy things and a snake . . . Okay, the snake wasn't dangerous and neither was the other stuff, was it? Really, some stones on the floor and some painted figures on the walls. Red walls. Pentagrams. Who does that?

Dammit, Beau, why didn't you warn me about this room? She pulled her cell phone out of her pocket and dialed his direct number.

"Ah, the Martinez place."

"Yes, dammit. The one filled with a bunch of scary shit. How could you have forgotten to mention it?"

"Calm down, Sam. I didn't actually see it. One of the other deputies went in there, said he didn't find anything related to the woman's death. He just described it as a weird room. Lot of old dusty stuff in there he said. I pictured something like an attic full of junk. Got another call and left. I'm sorry I didn't think to tell you about it."

Sam felt a little stupid. It really was just a room full of dusty old junk, when you thought about it.

"Can you handle it on your own?" he asked. He sounded genuinely concerned. "I could come out there later, if you want me to."

Now she *really* felt dumb. Nothing like being such a girl that she had to have the big old deputy sheriff with her before she could face down a dead snake. "No, that's okay. I was just startled. I can do it."

She put the phone back in her pocket and noticed that the rain had already slowed. *I can do it, I can do it.* She kept saying it as she walked back inside, convincing herself as much as anyone.

Sunlight broke through the clouds, giving a whole new

perspective to the house, as she walked through the living room. The rooms she'd cleaned were nice and bright, and the main bedroom felt quite benign now that Bertha's personal belongings were gone. With a square of late-afternoon sun on the floor, even the red room showed itself to be what Beau had described, a dusty collection of old things. Sam took up a broom and swept the white stones and bundled herbs into a harmless pile. The stiff snake went into a garbage bag. It was a little creepy, picking it up, but she handled it just fine. She dropped the black candles—so dusty that they were nearly gray, in the clear light of day—into the same bag with the snake. All of it went out to the bed of the pickup.

A stack of books in one corner showed titles pertaining to native American symbolism and beliefs, herbal treatments and such. Two of them specifically addressed witchcraft but even they didn't seem nearly as ominous now. She whipped the dust off of them with a cloth and carried the stack out to join the other books in her truck. There. All done. Alive to tell about it.

Alive and hungry. She locked up and headed off to meet her destiny at KFC.

Zoe stopped by around seven. Sam had showered off her coating of dust and whipped up the batter for her special lighter-than-air white cake. With raspberry and truffle cream filling, and her secret fresh-coconut frosting, the triple layer torte would be the highlight of the ladies luncheon for the Taos Heritage Foundation tomorrow. The three layers went into the oven and she sat at the kitchen table tallying her hours for the two properties she'd cleaned this week. It would add up to a decent amount and she hoped to bank at least half of it in her special account for the opening of Sweet's Sweets.

"Hey there! Knock-knock." Zoe called through the screen door and opened it at the same time. "Any more weird things happen today?"

Which? The artist's sketchbook hidden in the wall at the Anderson place, or the witchy room at Bertha Martinez's? Sam started to give the condensed version when Zoe spotted the carved wooden box at the other end of the table. Life had been nothing but weird this week.

"Oh, is this it?" Her eyes grew wide and she reached for the box.

"Careful. That thing is . . ." Sam wasn't sure quite how to describe it.

"Possessed?" Zoe joked.

"I don't know. It's got something."

She turned it over in her hands but didn't open it.

"I brought you some more strange stuff. I'll get it out of the truck in a minute." Sam hadn't bothered to deliver any of the collected junk from today's haul. "Some antique bottles with herbal *whatever* in them, some books on herbs and even a volume or two on witchcraft."

Zoe set the box down as if it was suddenly too hot to hold.

"Sam . . . do you really think that old woman was a *bruja*?"

"Never thought about it until I came across that red room at her house. I don't . . . I don't know much about any of that stuff, but aren't the *brujas* of Spanish tradition more . . . um . . ."

"They were often consulted for their healing powers."

She raised a foot and wiggled her toes.

"No. Forget it," Sam protested. She did *not* get hexed somehow by that old lady.

"The stories go every direction," Zoe said. "A lot of them seem to combine tales from all sorts of tradition—shamanism, Catholicism, voodoo. Many people believe *brujas* are shape-shifters. They can become an animal like a coyote or an owl."

"Or a snake?"

Chapter 9

The oven timer went off just then and Sam jumped up to check her cake layers. By the time she pulled them out and turned off the oven, Zoe was antsy to go. She'd left Darryl with the impression that she was bringing home ice cream and she still had to deliver on that promise. Sam poured her a little jar of fresh raspberry filling to use as a topping and they walked out to the driveway together. Sam retrieved the boxes of books and medicine bottles from the back seat of her truck and Zoe headed off, happy with her new treasures.

Sam watched her taillights retreat down the quiet lane, thinking how glad she would be to offload the rest of Bertha Martinez's stuff, with stops at the thrift shop and the county landfill. Her glance slid sideways to the trash bag that held the stuffed snake. Shape-shifter indeed.

Cake layers occupied her mind for a few more minutes, as she removed them from the pans and laid them out on cooling racks. While they cooled she blended the truffle cream filling for one of the layers, and cooked the raspberry syrup down until it was thick and spreadable for the other layer. The best thing about baking was that little tasks like grating fresh coconut were the perfect way to relax and escape all of the day's other stresses. Before she knew it, she had more than double what she needed for the coconut frosting. Into the fridge, it would be there for something else.

While the layers cooled completely, Sam brought her laptop computer to the table and did a little research on the artist, Pierre Cantone. A search brought up at least a dozen websites devoted to his work and she knew this was more than she could absorb that night. She bookmarked the ones that seemed most interesting and turned back to assembling the torte before exhaustion overtook her.

Sam woke up early, probably because she'd completely crashed around nine o'clock. Today would be a busy one and that, too, contributed to the fact that she was staring wide-eyed at a clock which said it was 5:38.

Over coffee she took up her research on Pierre Cantone where she'd left off last night. The artist, born in 1937, raised in Provence, was best known for the amazing quality of light and shadow that he brought to an otherwise-fuzzy impressionistic style. He'd come onto the art scene when Picasso was grabbing all the attention with cubism, just a young wannabe when tastes were moving away from the style so popular a generation earlier. But Cantone ploughed onward and garnered, if not critical praise, popular attention. The elite called him a hack but buyers flocked to him. By the time Picasso died in 1973, Cantone was at the top of his game. Then tragedy struck.

His lovely wife Adele and their two children died in a train derailment, the only three fatalities when hundreds of other passengers escaped nearly unscathed. It crushed Cantone. Ranting against the world for the gross unfairness of it, he took to drinking heavily and he stopped painting. A corrupt business manager may have raided the successful artist's life savings—no one seemed to know. The man disappeared, leaving Cantone living alone in a squalid New York tenement, in poverty.

At some point the Frenchman met a woman, another artist who raved about the art scene in New Mexico. Georgia O'Keefe was living there. Perhaps Cantone would be newly inspired if he were to meet the great lady artist. The record was never clear on whether this woman was a lover or simply a friend with Cantone's best interests at heart, but she did carry enough influence to convince him to give New Mexico a try. He moved to Santa Fe and lived in the guesthouse of a patron. But, sadly, his work was never the same and he barely produced enough to live on. Then he vanished.

Sam followed other links in the search but everything written about Cantone seemed to agree. No one knew where the artist went after a dozen or so years in Santa Fe. He'd either died ignominiously or simply dropped out of public life. Since then, of course, his remaining known works had skyrocketed in value, with several of them bringing high six-figures at auction. She studied photos of the paintings and felt her pulse quicken. The little mural they'd found was certainly in the same style, and yet it was not a duplicate of any of Cantone's known works. Had she found Cantone's mysterious hiding place? And where was he now?

She would probably never know the answers, but she'd drained two cups of coffee by this time and was antsy to get on with the day. By nine a.m. she was on her way to the landfill with the bags of trash from the Martinez place (never so glad to see something thrown away as when she tossed the snake bag over the edge). The few useful items went to the thrift shop on her way back into town and she popped back by her house to pick up the raspberry torte and deliver it to the Taos Heritage place just as the women were beginning to arrive for their luncheon.

Declining a half-hearted invitation to stay for their lunch and presentation (really, did they want her here fresh from the landfill?), she picked up a sack of tacos at Taco Bell and headed back home. They were going to the soggy side by the time she finished unloading the truck—no sense in cleaning herself up twice. She washed her hands of the dust and carefully placed Pierre Cantone's sketchbook out of harm's way on the kitchen table. Beside Bertha's old wooden box, the two items looked like a pair of artifacts from another era.

Sam downed three tacos without blinking and chided herself for not being a more conscious eater. How was she ever going to lose the spare pounds? She crushed the paper sack with the two remaining tacos and threw them in the trash, like that would make any real difference before tonight's dinner with Beau Cardwell. But as long as she was feeling a little bit virtuous she also poured out the soda she'd bought and drew a glass of fresh water from the tap.

The phone rang and she flinched. Zoe would be happy to lecture her on the evils of fast food and too much sugar, eating habits being the one source of contention between them, but a glance at the caller ID told her it was Rupert instead. Now there was a man who would never give you a hard time about calories. In his mind butter is one of the essential food groups.

"Hey Rupert, what's up?"

"Honey, I got twenty-three pages written today, which is a real miracle because I can hardly concentrate on work. Esteban sent some photos of the mural to New York and they are *very* excited. I mean, *very*. He's crating up the painting today and shipping it out for authentication. If we have a real Cantone here, it's going to be such a boost for Taos. I mean, that's proof positive that he lived here, right *here* in our little town."

Considering that several famous artists and writers lived here over the years, it's not like this one thing would put Taos on the map. But it would still be exciting news.

"I read up a little, this morning, but Cantone's history gets blurry at the end. No one seems to know where he went or what he did. If he's still alive, he should get the mural back, or get the money when it sells. And if he's not living, I wonder if there are relatives. Maybe there's a will." Sam had to pause for a breath. "Do you know of any way to find out?"

"I'll ask around in the art community. If Cantone lived here for awhile, maybe someone in town knew him."

Sam hung up, feeling a little guilty that she'd not told Rupert about the sketchbook. It was certainly a treasure and further evidence that the mural was genuine. But somehow she didn't want to talk about it quite yet. Meanwhile, she was still curious about the body buried on the property. Was it Anderson, the homeowner, or was it the younger man who'd lived with him? And how did he die? She shook off the thoughts. It might have been someone else entirely, and even though the grave looked fresh to Sam maybe it wasn't; maybe the burial happened years ago.

So, what to do with the sketchbook in the meantime? She gathered it, and the wooden box, and carried them to her bedroom. Since no one knew of the existence of the sketches, she decided she could get by with stashing the book between her mattress and foundation. That wasn't going to be good enough for the long term and she would probably have to end up either turning it over to the authorities or renting a safe deposit box at the bank. But for now, it would do.

The puff-textured wooden box sat on the bedspread, staring at her. She placed her hands on the sides of it. The wood was cool to the touch, the cabochon stones dull in color. She closed her eyes and ran her hands over the smoothly rounded mounds of the quilted sections. The surface immediately warmed. Whoa. Her eyes popped open; her fingers tingled.

Did she imagine it, or were the stones brighter? The blue, red and green pieces were nearly glowing. The wood surface also seemed different, with a golden patina to it, a softer, nicer color than the previous sickly yellow. When Sam brought it home she thought she would work on it with some polish, but now it shone as if she'd already done that. She looked at her hands. Did body oils have the ability to polish wood? Nah. Not like this.

She wiped her hands on the tail of her shirt and picked up the box. Maybe it would look nice on the dresser. She could use it as a jewelry box. She set it in place and stepped back to admire it. Yes. That was a good spot for it. She lifted the lid. The stiff hinges creaked, as before, but as she closed and reopened it a couple of times they loosened considerably. Soon, the lid was operating as smoothly as if she'd just applied oil.

"You're a strange little thing," she said. "What is your secret?"

Chapter 10

The phone rang, startling Sam, and she set the box back in place on the dresser.

"Hi Sam," said Beau. "I, uh . . . this sounds weird but I just had the strongest urge to call you."

She stared at the wooden box, its colors dimming now.

"What I meant was, I thought I'd check to see if we're still on for dinner tonight?"

"Sure." She grimaced. No matter what he said, it felt like that awkward first-date stuff. What shall I wear? Where are we going? And of course, the other awkward question—where might this lead? Her past was checkered with too many first dates, too many one-night stands. The past few years had brought a certain freedom from that as she'd steered away from dating and concentrated on building her business and enjoying her solitude.

"Are you afraid of heights?" he asked, pulling her back to the present.

She laughed out loud at the unexpected question. "No, actually, I'm not."

"I know this spot at the Rio Grande Gorge. Away from the bridge where all the tourists stop. We can drive to this pullout I know and then walk a little way, and there's a flat rock ledge that is a great place to watch a sunset. If that sounds good to you, I can pick you up around six?"

"Perfect." She hung up, completely relieved that he hadn't suggested some romantic dress-up place, not that Taos had a lot of those anyway. Wherever they ate dinner, walking around on rocky terrain ahead of time was going to require comfortable shoes and casual clothing. She surveyed her closet and pulled out her best-fitting pair of jeans and a top that concealed the bulges she wanted concealed. She chided herself for trying to think ahead about any relationship with Beau. How silly. He undoubtedly had every hungry woman in town under fifty chasing after him. Sam knew she had to be at least five years older than he, and not a prize in the looks department. This was a friendship thing, a shared interest in a couple of abandoned houses. That's all. That's all she wanted.

She repeated it to herself three times.

Nevertheless, when she started to dress for the evening she found herself applying fresh eye makeup and adding a touch of gloss over the rose colored lipstick that was her normal shade. She even debated polishing her nails, but the past two days of scrubbing and hauling trash had taken their toll in ragged, broken ones so she opted for filing them down smooth and massaging in a lot of cuticle cream.

He showed up promptly, driving a blue Ford Explorer rather than the department vehicle. Gentlemanly to the core, he removed his Stetson as he approached her door and rang the bell. She knew this because she watched through the sheer drapes at the living room window. She chided herself for doing it, and let a full ten seconds go by before opening the door.

The ride through town and out to the gorge was filled with that inane 'how was your day' chitchat which seems to mark the beginning of new friendships that don't yet have enough momentum to simply pick up where the last conversation ended. Sam told Beau about Rupert's excitement over the mural's being sent to New York for authentication. And this time she mentioned the sketchbook.

"How would that work?" she asked. "Does the book go with the house, or does it belong to Cantone?"

"Depends. If Cantone accidentally left it behind, I imagine he or his heirs might make a case for it belonging to him. On the other hand, Anderson—or his heirs—might make an equally good case for abandonment of the book. Or they might say that Cantone gifted the book to Anderson. Most likely it would end up belonging to the current home owner, Anderson."

"He might be forced to sell assets to satisfy the mortgage too."

"There's that," he agreed. "I'll probably have autopsy results by tomorrow. If the body turns out to be Anderson, then we have to start looking in that direction for next of kin."

Sam sat silently, contemplating that, while Beau pulled off the road and steered toward a little clear spot where he parked the SUV.

"This is it."

She stood beside the vehicle, letting the breeze ruffle the short layers of her hair, while he got something from the back.

"Dinner," he said, holding up a picnic basket. He handed it to her, while he carried a folded quilt and an industrial-sized flashlight. "Once that sun goes down it's going to get pretty dark out here."

She followed him down a narrow path that obviously didn't see much traffic, to a rock ledge which was only about ten feet square. From the edge of it the earth fell away, a rocky field that went straight down eight hundred feet. The Rio Grande Gorge is a deep cut through volcanic rock, maybe a half-mile wide at the top, with the silvery ribbon of the Rio Grande River coursing through the bottom. Sam stood near enough to the edge to peer down at it and took a deep breath of sage and piñon, pungent from the afternoon rain.

"I like this spot because the wind isn't so fierce here," Beau said. "Out on the bridge you sometimes feel like you'll get carried away."

It was true. The way the surrounding cliff walls rose, they were in a sheltered spot and yet the western view was clear and she could see that the sun would dip to the level of the distant volcanoes in another hour or so.

"It's so beautiful. And quiet!"

"Get this." He faced the drop-off and let out a cowboy whoop. It echoed back, crossed the distance again, and reverberated off the rocky walls to fill the air with sound.

"I love it!" Her shriek rang back in triplicate.

He sent a musical Laaaaa . . . out over the chasm. As it began to echo back Sam gave a strong harmonic note of her own. He raised it. She raised him again. The music that filled the air sounded like a choir of hundreds. She felt her eyes widen at the magic of it. When she looked at him, his reaction was the same. He held her gaze as the sound faded.

"Wow." It came out in a whisper. "Do musicians come out here and do this all the time?"

He shook his head. "I don't think so. It's our secret." He reached out and raised her chin and gave her a very soft kiss.

She blinked a couple of times. What the—

He stepped back. "Sam, I'm sorry. I didn't intend that— I don't mean to push you—"

She shook her head, dismissing the apology. "It's . . . it's okay. It was a special moment." It meant nothing. But why were her insides all fluttery?

He flashed her a killer smile. "Hungry?"

Oh boy. She wasn't sure how to answer that one. Yes. In every possible way.

But she saw that he'd turned to the picnic basket and was pulling out a bottle of wine and a little plastic container. *Keep it light, Sam.*

"I'm afraid I'm no gourmet cook," he said. "This is just your basic cowboy dinner."

Well, hardly, she thought. The plastic tub contained guacamole dip and he pointed to a bag of corn chips. "Hold this," he said, handing her the items while he whipped the quilt out and brought it to rest on the rocky ground. Then he rummaged in the basket and came up with a corkscrew. She watched him study it for a minute and then offered to open the wine if he would find glasses.

"Oops. I knew I would forget something."

"Hey, I've drunk almost as much wine directly from the bottle as from a glass," she said. Memories of cheap Thunderbird and Boone's Farm.

To prove it, she tossed the cork onto the blanket and took a swig. A macho wipe across the lips with the back of her hand and she offered the bottle over to him. They passed it back and forth a few times, watching the sun on its downward course.

"What else is in that basket?"

He pulled out an insulated container about a gallon in size. "Chile—my specialty. Uh, I think I forgot bowls, though. But there are spoons." He held them up with a grin that gave her an excellent picture of what he'd looked like as an eight year old.

Sam ripped open the bag of corn chips, took one and scooped up guacamole with it. "Did you make this? It's really good."

He blushed a little. "Should I admit that I found the recipe on the internet? It was the only one that used two ingredients so I thought I could handle it."

"It's great!"

"Now the chile—that's my own recipe. Sorta. My mama used to make it. She doesn't cook anymore, so I make it for her. After I moved to New Mexico I started adding green chile to it. I mean, you really can't live here and not eat green chile, right?"

They sat cross legged on the quilt with the Thermos between them, spoons at the ready as he unscrewed the lid and released a bouquet of meaty, tomatoey, spicy goodness into the air. They dipped their spoons at the same moment.

"Ohmygod, that's good." Sam had to admit she'd never had chile that tasty—either in New Mexico or back home in Texas. A moan escaped her.

He grinned and went for a second spoonful. She did

the same.

"Try it this way," he said. He grabbed a few corn chips and tossed them onto the chile, then spooned up a big bite that included a couple of them. Sam did the same and agreed. Heaven.

"You could cook for me any time," she said, once she got the chance to take a breath.

"You'd have to like chile a whole lot. This and grilled cheese sandwiches are about the only things I can make."

The idea of this chile *and* a grilled cheese sandwich nearly made her swoon. The sun dropped below the horizon, leaving the silhouettes of black volcanic cones and turning the few clouds into every shade of flame. Cicadas droned their metallic stridulation in the soft dusk.

"I could die this very minute and be happy," she told him.

"Well, we'll hope that doesn't happen."

"You know what I mean." She took another hit from the wine bottle and passed it over. "I feel so lucky right now. What a spectacular evening."

"I'm glad you like the spot. I was afraid you might have been hoping for a restaurant dinner, some fancy place. Course I worried about it a little too late, after I already had the basket loaded up."

"Beau, it's just right. Absolutely perfect." And it was. She couldn't think of a more relaxed, fun way to get to know him better. She would *not* call it a date, and she would do her best to ignore that kiss.

They finished off the chips and dip, made a good-sized dent in the quantity of chile, and were sipping at the last of the wine when his phone rang. Okay, an almost perfect evening.

He glanced at the readout. "OMI's office. I better take this."

Sam leaned back on her elbows and stretched her legs out as he conversed quietly. The first star showed in the east and soon there were a dozen of them.

"Sorry. I knew Archie was hustling to get the autopsy finished tonight so he could take the whole weekend off. He wanted to let me know the gist of it."

"Can you tell me?"

"It's Riley Anderson. Hair from a brush in the master bedroom matches the body's DNA. Archie is ruling natural causes. There was lots of lung congestion, no wounds or trauma. Probably untreated pneumonia, which he says is consistent with an age-related death."

"So, now what? Do you find relatives of Mr. Anderson? Bury him back on the property or what?"

"I'm not sure."

"Since he was in default on his mortgage, the USDA has the power to auction off the property, so someone else will soon own it. Are they going to want a stranger's body buried in their back yard?"

"Probably not. I guess the answer is to find him a spot in the public cemetery. Technically, a pauper's grave. Unless someone comes along who can claim kinship and then they can make their own arrangements."

"What about the guy who was living with him?" Sam asked. "The neighbor hinted that they might have had a relationship."

"You talked to the neighbors?" He gave her a firm stare.

"The last time I was there a lady named Betty McDonald

came walking up. I just kind of let her ramble on."

"I'll run some background on Anderson," he said. "See if we can track down someone."

The sky was completely dark now and at least a billion stars were visible, out here away from town. Sam felt she could be content to stare up at them all night but could tell that Beau was getting restless. It was time to call it a night and go home. They used the big flashlight to be sure they'd left nothing behind, then stowed the picnic gear in the Explorer.

"I sure didn't want to cut the evening short," he said as he turned into her drive. "But I'm on duty early tomorrow and I'd like to stop off and get that autopsy report they faxed over so I can look at it yet tonight."

"Hey, duty calls. I understand." She, too, had work planned for the morning.

Chapter 11

Sam awoke Saturday morning feeling lazy. At the suggestion of Delbert Crow, she'd planned to dash over to Bertha Martinez's place one last time and apply a couple coats of neutral paint to the walls in the red room. He was right, the house would stand a better chance of selling quickly without strange symbols painted on red walls. She'd have probably done it in the first place but needed an okay to lay out money for refurbishment on a property.

Now, she lounged in bed for an extra thirty minutes reliving the picnic dinner and last night's beautiful setting. Maybe the extra wine was making her lazy today. Maybe the niggling thought that a fling with Beau Cardwell might not be such a bad thing . . . just maybe, that was the source of her unaccustomed languor.

After awhile she couldn't postpone getting to work. She rummaged in the closet for her painting jeans, the ones that had already met with the touch of a brush, and an old shirt.

Her hair was too short to gather into a ponytail but she decided a bandana over it might help keep it out of her face during the job. She stashed her watch and the favorite opal ring that she usually wore into her new jewelry box. Again, she swore that the stones on it glowed more brightly after she'd touched the box.

A quick stop at the hardware store for two gallons of paint and she was headed out to the Martinez place. The red bedroom felt less ominous this time, with sun shining in the window and all the weird artifacts gone. In no time at all, she'd pulled down the heavy drapes and hardware and began rolling paint onto the dark walls. As expected, it would need at least two coats, but the stuff dried quickly and by the time she finished the fourth wall the first was about dry enough. She stopped for a granola bar and cup of coffee from the Thermos she'd brought. The second coat went on even more quickly and the trim work was minimal. She glanced at her wrist but remembered that she'd left her watch at home. Not that it mattered.

She bagged up the throwaway paint roller set and the empty cans and set them out for garbage collection, locked the house and was on her way.

Back at home a message on the machine told Sam that the Casa de Tranquilidad spa near Santa Fe wanted eight dozen specialty cookies for a reception. She'd worked with them before, supplying cakes and pastries for different events. Driving down there to deliver was a little bit of a hassle but they paid well and it was a way to get her business name out in front of a whole new clientele. She returned the call, got the details, and inventoried her supply of ingredients. Wrote up a little shopping list. Before she quite made it to the door the phone rang again.

"Hey, Rupert, what's up?"

"Girl, I can't write a word today. I'm just in such a whirl over the big find."

"You haven't heard back from the appraiser in New York already, have you?"

"Oh, no. They've probably just received the piece. They'll need a few days at least."

"I'm just on my way out to the store. Can we chat a little later?" Sam explained about the big cookie order.

"Can I come with you?" He sounded so eager that she couldn't say no. And he might actually be of help. Rupert was pretty efficient in the kitchen. Maybe she could get him to operate the cookie press while she decorated or something like that. His place was right on the way so she told him she'd pick him up in ten minutes.

They were standing in the checkout line at Smith's when her cell rang. Beau.

"Would it be convenient for you to stop by my office on Civic Plaza at some point today?" he asked. "I've finished with Anderson's personal papers and thought you might need to include them with the other contents of the home."

Normally she didn't keep papers from the homeowners, but in this case she could offer to hold onto or dispose of them, whatever was required.

"How about in five minutes? I'm nearly there now."

Rupert decided to go inside with her. "If you're dating this guy, I need to pay more attention."

Sam bristled. "It was *not* a date, big brother."

They found parking right next to the building, which was some kind of miracle, and were directed to Beau's cubicle down a narrow corridor. His desk was fairly neat, considering the amount of paperwork even the most minor case required these days. A number of file folders stood upright between the dividers in an organizer caddy. In the center of the desk one folder lay spread open and he was tamping some pages and stapling the corner of them as they walked up.

Beau handed her a rubber-banded stack of envelopes that she recognized as the bank statements she'd collected from the house. Their fingers touched briefly as she took them, and she got the feeling that his request for her to get these items was an excuse to see her.

She glanced toward the open folder on the desk. Clipped to the front was a DMV photo of a gray-haired man.

"Is that Mr. Anderson?"

Beau nodded and pulled the picture from the paperclip, handing it to her.

"Ohmygod—it's him!" Rupert snatched the photo from Sam. His breath was coming hard.

"Him?"

"It's Cantone! He's older here, but I'd know that face anywhere."

Beau stepped forward. "You're sure? Absolutely sure?"

Sam looked at it more closely. The photos of the artist that she'd seen online were mostly taken in the 1960s and '70s at the height of his career. He'd been dark haired then, with a pencil mustache and smooth face. In the DMV photo he was gray, no facial hair, with severe bags under the eyes. Cruel, what time did to everyone.

However, the more she looked, the more resemblance she could see. He wore his hair in essentially the same style, combed straight back, longish, touching his collar. Although the official photo was straight-on, whereas the publicity photos were generally posed at a more flattering angle, the bone structure was the same.

"I'm telling you . . ." Rupert said.

"Yes, I can see it too," she told Beau. "Check online. There's a lot of information about the artist. I think it's him."

She handed the photo back and Beau clipped it to the file.

"Well, this adds a new wrinkle. Surely there must be someone related . . . I mean, it wouldn't be right to put him in a pauper's grave now, would it?"

Rupert inhaled sharply. "For Cantone? You *have* to be joking."

"Well, we didn't know—"

"I will personally pay for a grand funeral for this man before I'll let you just stick him—" He actually began to tear up.

Sam laid her hand on his arm. "Rupert, it's okay. Now that we know who he is . . . It's going to be okay."

Beau spoke up. "Rupert, that's very kind of you. But now that we know his identity, we have to make an attempt at locating next of kin. Once we know if he has living relatives, decisions can be made."

"I'm sure you can be part of the plans, Rupert, once his relatives are found."

He visibly relaxed. Rupert loved to plan a party and Sam could already see the cogs turning.

Beau said, "You know a lot about this man's life, Rupert. Do you know if he had children?"

Rupert told Beau the same story Sam had discovered online, that the artist's wife and children were killed in a train crash years earlier. He'd never remarried and had become quite reclusive. Adopting a fake identity was about as anonymous as a person could get, Sam imagined.

She spoke up: "I'm wondering about the younger man who was living with him. According to Betty McDonald he showed up in March and was gone—well, both men were gone—in June. I wonder if he was related. Anderson, uh, Cantone, didn't seem like the type of guy to have a stranger move in with him."

"I seem to remember a brother . . . or maybe it was a sister," Rupert said. "Let me check." He pulled out his cell phone and dialed a number from memory.

"Esteban. Hey, Rupert here. What do you know of any family history on Pierre Cantone?" He listened and hmm'd a couple of times. For a couple of minutes he simply waited, as the other man talked. "Okay. Thanks ever so."

"Okay, here's the deal." Rupert loved to tell a story and he was just warming up.

Beau picked up on that and pulled a couple of chairs closer to his desk so they could sit down during the telling.

"Cantone had a sister. Sophie. She was ten years younger. She married an American, an older man—really a romantic whirlwind thing during a trip to New York." He sighed. "Kind of like the scenario I created in *Love's Glory* where—"

Sam tapped his foot with her toe.

"—oh, right. Sophie Cantone became Mrs. Robert Killington. He was wealthy, an industrialist or something. They had the most to-die-for apartment in New York, right on Central Park, and a villa in the south of France."

She could see Beau's eyes beginning to glaze over.

"Children?" she reminded.

"Ah yes. Esteban wasn't sure. He thought he remembered there being a son, but if so the child was kept completely out of the limelight. Sophie and Robert traveled the world and attended all the right parties and there were never any children in sight."

Beau stood, a clear signal. "That gives us a lot to go on. Thanks, Rupert."

Sam nudged Rupert in the shoulder to remind him that they needed to get moving.

"I'll do some checking to see if Sophie and Robert Killington are still living. As his sister, she—"

"Oh, they aren't," Rupert interrupted. "Living. That's what else I meant to say. He died after only about ten years of marriage. He was quite a lot older, remember. She stayed around the art scene, attending many openings as Cantone's hostess, for a few years more. But then she became ill—the rumor was cancer. She died only five or six years after her husband. It was so tragic. So young."

"Then I guess I'll start with the possibility that the son might still be living. Maybe even in Europe," Beau said.

Rupert and Sam left him to the search. His phone was already ringing as they walked down the corridor.

"Sam, let's dash back out there. To Cantone's house? Please?"

She unlocked the truck. "Oh, Rupert, I've got all those cookies to bake . . ." And she wanted his help. She would get that a whole lot easier if she didn't send him into a pout. "All right, but just a few minutes, okay?"

He seemed as delighted as a kid going to the carnival. The Anderson/Cantone place was only about fifteen minutes away. Sam was surprised to see that it was just a little past noon, anyway. She'd accomplished a lot already today so it shouldn't matter that they take a quick side trip.

Rupert was beaming as she unlocked the door to the simple wood frame house. While he clearly regarded this as a near-shrine, knowing that his beloved artist had lived here, Sam merely saw it as sad, that such a respected man had ended up unable to pay for even this worn-down abode.

He headed straight for the front bedroom, where they'd found the art supplies and where the mural was painted. Even with it gone and the wall patched, Rupert seemed to sense the essence of the artist at work in the cramped space. Sam, meanwhile, went to the kitchen, updating her sign-in sheet, making sure that she'd left everything in order for the pending sale of the place.

At once she sensed something different. What was this greenish, powdery stuff on the wall near the table? And there—more of it near the sink. She'd wiped down the counter and table with disinfectant cleaner. She could see her circular wipe marks in dried swirls of green. No way she left it like this. She checked the back door. Still locked tight.

"What's going on?" Rupert asked, peering around the doorjamb.

"Huh?"

"You cursed. I heard you say 'what the f—' all the way down the hall."

"Look at this!" She pointed to the table. "I didn't leave all that green stuff."

"Uh-huh. Sam, there's no green stuff."

"Right there!" She flicked her fingers toward the wall. "And there. Powdery stuff on the wall. Swipe marks on the table."

He was staring at her blankly.

"Stop it! No teasing." She laughed but it came out sort of shaky. "Rupert, you're scaring me. You do see this." She wiped her finger across it and some of the green came off. She held it up to him.

"Honey, I see a table and a kitchen that looks perfectly clean. You'd never leave a mess behind in one of your places. You clean like the devil when you do these jobs."

Sam felt like she'd been whacked. What the hell was going on? She rubbed at her eyes and blinked hard. The green stuff was still there. And her good friend was looking at her like she'd just sprouted horns.

"I want a third opinion." She pulled out her phone and dialed Beau. No answer on his cell. Sam stopped herself. How crazy would it sound, trying to explain this to him?

Rupert was watching her from the doorway.

"You. Keep out of this," she grumbled. He flinched and slinked away.

She stomped across the kitchen and flung the door open. It closed behind her, a lot more firmly than she'd intended. She strode over to the gaping hole in the back corner and stared into the empty grave for a good ten minutes. Maybe she *was* going crazy. Maybe not. But snapping at her friends wouldn't solve anything.

She took a deep breath and headed back to the house.

Refusing to look closely at the kitchen walls, Sam went back to the bedroom where Rupert was sitting on the bed, looking like a whipped puppy. "Hey, I'm sorry. I shouldn't have yelled at you." She sat down beside him.

"And I shouldn't have doubted you. That's not what friends do." He took her hand.

"So, we're good?"

"We're good." He patted her hand and gave it a light squeeze. "Want some help with those cookies?"

"Absolutely. I'll just recheck all the locks first."

He went out to the truck while Sam made the rounds, ignoring the green powder in several places. She rinsed her fingers at the kitchen sink and the substance came right off. So strange.

She drove back home, still shaky over the fact that she was seeing things other people couldn't see, hoping that it wasn't some alien concoction from the Planet Whatever.

Chapter 12

By two o'clock Rupert and Sam were up to their elbows in cookies. He'd completely moved past the earlier little tiff and pitched in with his practiced ease in the kitchen. As Sam mixed each new flavor of dough he operated the press and filled cookie sheets with neat rows of butter cookies, chocolate spritz, butter-mint whirls and more. She shuffled them in and out of the oven and onto cooling racks. As he worked up the final batch she prepared decorator icing and began piping a variety of tiny summer flowers onto the cooled ones. She loved to see how many different styles she could come up with, customizing every order so the customer always received a surprise.

A tap at the kitchen door caught her attention. Zoe turned the knob and came in.

"Hey. You guys must be way into your own zone," she said. "I knocked at the front door twice. Figured you had to be here since your truck is out front."

Sam gestured toward the counters and table, which were covered with racks of cookies at various stages of completion.

"Quick question and I'll leave you alone," Zoe said. "Can I borrow your truck tomorrow, for the day? Darryl's just informed me that he's working and needs his truck, and I have some furniture to take to the library's garage sale fundraiser. I told them I'd also help haul away anything that doesn't sell by five o'clock. They donate it to the homeless shelter."

"Ooh. I have to get all these cookies delivered to Santa Fe."

She leaned against the counter, wheels turning. "How about we trade vehicles? Can you fit all the cookies into my Subaru wagon?"

"That'll work."

"Let's just trade keys now. Sounds like we'll both be done by early evening and we can switch back then."

Sam wiped frosting off her hands, fetched the truck keys from her backpack and got Zoe on her way. The rest of the baking operation went smoothly and she was surprised to see that it was only four o'clock as she started clearing the mixing bowls and putting the utensils to soak in the sink.

"You, girl, sure know how to roar through an order," Rupert commented, plopping into one of the kitchen chairs. "I'm beat."

She stared around the room. They'd accomplished an amazing amount of baking in a short time, and the results were stacked everywhere. "Thank goodness for triple-decked racks," she said. "This kitchen is so inadequate."

"Hey, you'll get your shop. My offer still stands."

He'd generously proposed to loan Sam the money to properly open Sweet's Sweets. She had to admit that it was tempting to take him up on it. But she also knew that opening a retail store was a risky thing. There would be a lot of expenses that she couldn't foresee, and she'd feel better if she could at least foot most of the bill herself, without the worry of repaying a loan. A flash of irritation, again, at her daughter for helping herself to the savings Sam had so carefully accumulated. She suppressed it and turned on a flame under the tea kettle.

"I think we can spare a few of these little beauties and have ourselves a proper tea," she told Rupert, handing him a plate.

He chose an assortment of the cookies and she poured them each a cup of Earl Grey.

Sam woke up Sunday morning feeling satisfied. After she'd taken Rupert home—he swore that the cookies had given him renewed energy to get back to his writing—she'd pulled out disposable platters and carefully arranged the cookies in two nice displays, topping them with plastic covers. They'd made a couple dozen extras, just in case, and she made up a few sampler baggies. It never hurt to throw in a few gifts along the way.

After a slow-paced morning at home she loaded up her treasures and headed for Santa Fe. The hour and a half drive went smoothly, the only traffic snags coming as she approached the northern edge of the capital city, where weekends brought crowds out to the flea market. By then she was watching for the turnoff to Casa de Tranquilidad, where she followed a winding gravel road to the hotel resort. The meandering adobe building sat at an overlook, surrounded by pine forest. Really a beautiful spot for conferences or weddings or social events. Sam hoped her effort on the cookies would bring even more business from them.

She pulled under the portico at the front entrance, unsure which meeting room was her destination. The hotel's conference coordinator usually suggested she avoid the bustle of the kitchen, as long as the client's meeting room was available. She made a quick inquiry at the front desk, got her instructions and headed back to the car. The valet parking attendant seemed a bit impatient at the length of time she'd parked and she felt pressure to stack the trays and carry them both at once. About the time she'd nearly dumped one of them a young woman with long auburn hair came walking up. She looked like a hotel guest, carrying a leather duffle, and she noticed Sam's plight.

"Could I help you with those?" she asked, dropping her bag near the Subaru.

Sam gladly handed off one of the trays. "Thanks. It wasn't smart for me to try handling both of them."

She followed Sam inside and they set down their burdens. Back at the car the younger woman picked up her duffle, introducing herself as Charlie Parker.

"Here, Charlie, let me . . ." Sam reached for the samples she'd bagged up. "If you ever need pastries, give me a call."

She looked at Sam's card and thanked her, eyeing the cookies—obviously a girl who liked her sweets, although her slender figure belied that. Sam gave her a smile and then caught the eye of the valet who was clearly sending annoyance vibes her way. She climbed back into the car as Charlie went into the lobby.

Sam stopped in Espanola for a quick burger and reached the outskirts of Taos as it was getting dark. Her cell phone rang about two seconds after she'd traded Zoe's Subaru back for her pickup truck, Beau asking if she'd like to meet for dinner. She explained about the burger and he sounded so disappointed that she caved and said she'd love an ice cream.

They decided that the Sonic Drive-in on the south side of town could satisfy both his need for solid food and her ice cream desires. She headed that way and had just pulled in when she spotted his Explorer behind her. He parked it at the side of the property and Sam pulled in at one of the slots with the old-time speakers for ordering. He climbed into her truck and they stared at the menu and placed their orders.

"I'm glad you were available on short notice," he said, sending a genuine smile her way. "This way it's not officially a date."

She sent him a saucy grin and told him about the delivery in Santa Fe. "You caught me just at the right moment. Otherwise, I'd have been snug inside."

He gave her a long, intent gaze. "Sam, I . . ."

Before he could finish the thought, a girl arrived with their tray. In the exchange of wrapped food, drinks, and cash, Beau took charge and Sam simply accepted her hot fudge sundae and watched as he unwrapped his chicken sandwich.

"Is there anything new on Cantone's death?"

"Not yet. Still waiting on some lab results." He turned sideways in his seat to face her. "But I don't want to think about work right now."

She'd set her empty sundae dish in the cup holder between them and he reached over to run a gentle finger down her forearm. He'd hardly taken two bites of his sandwich.

"Sam, I don't really know how to say this, so I'll just say it. I'm incredibly attracted to you."

She blushed and fiddled with a wadded napkin.

"You're a sexy lady, Sam. Don't you see that?"

"Ha!" It had been a whole lot of years since she'd seen herself as sexy. She met his gaze. "What is it that you see in me, really? I mean, you are this incredibly attractive man who could be dating fashion models, or at least women who are a lot younger and are built like fashion models. Why me?"

He reached over and squeezed her hand. "I love your smile, the way you laugh so easily, your energy. I've dated enough empty-headed, self-centered, beautiful women to know that they are a waste of my time."

"Really?" She'd never met a man like Beau who felt that way.

"The kiss the other night at the gorge was really nice . . ."

Now she knew she was blushing furiously. She glanced around at the other cars but no one seemed to be noticing them. And she had to agree; his kisses were the kind that sent lusty surges through her.

"So . . . could we go to your place?" he said.

All her common sense talk rushed at her. *It's too soon in the relationship. Is he genuine or is he using me? Am I really attracted to him?* The thoughts lasted a good five seconds. It wasn't as if she hadn't had casual sex before—just not in a whole lot of years. And maybe with Beau it would be more than casual. What would it hurt?

"Let's go," she said.

He got out of the truck and followed her through town, parking on the street. Sam pulled into her driveway, feeling the flush of desire and anticipation.

Then she noticed something else.

Parked in the wide turnaround spot at the back of her drive was a car. A shiny new Mustang convertible. Kelly.

Her daughter.

Chapter 13

Beau came walking up, just as she cut the truck's engine and got out. She waved helplessly at the red car. His face collapsed into the same *oh shit* expression that Sam imagined on her own.

"I have no idea what she's doing here," she said. "She lives in L.A. and only visits me when—"

"When there's trouble," he finished. "I'll go. You sort it out and call me later. Let me know if you need any help."

He gave her a lingering kiss and walked down the driveway.

Sam knew she should have expected this. Kelly had borrowed her bank balance a few weeks ago. That was the warning, the clue that should have let her know that her daughter would show up on her doorstep.

She walked to the back door, dreading the conversation that was about to take place.

Kelly, the girl who alternately charms my heart and wrenches my guts, Sam thought. *The young woman who should be out on her own—she's thirty-four years old, after all—but who shows up uninvited at the worst possible times.*

She paused at the door, the past flooding back. Thirty-five years ago Samantha Sweet had been this dumb girl just out of high school in small town Texas, seeing no future whatsoever in her job at the Dairy Queen. Billy Roy Farmer, from a long line of cotton-farming Farmers, was sniffing around like a horny dog. They'd lost their virginity together but truthfully Sam just couldn't see herself settling into a life of Tupperware parties, Friday night football games, Wednesdays and Sundays at the Baptist church, and forever looking out a kitchen window at miles of *flat*. Cause that's what a cotton farm in Texas was—flat.

Her life would become her mother's, and at night in the room Sam shared with her sister Rayleen, she'd nearly scream out loud at the thought of it. To keep from going entirely insane she thought of other places she might go, but truthfully, nobody she'd ever known had ever traveled any farther than Dallas so she didn't have much to compare to. In the 1970s a trip to Six Flags Over Texas was every local kid's idea of a dream come true.

Then one day she'd just taken her paycheck—$52.47 after taxes—and put half of it into her precious little savings account, which totaled nearly three hundred bucks after two summers and about a million Saturdays of making chocolate sundaes. She was on her way to the library to return a Kathleen Woodiwiss romance novel (that sort of reading was going to get her into trouble with Billy Roy, she just knew it). She knew there was such a thing as birth control, but Kathleen's characters never bothered with it and Sam was a little fuzzy on the details of how it worked anyway—they didn't discuss it much in the Baptist church.

Anyway, walking down Main Street, she passed Bobbie Jo Hudson's Travel Agency and a shiny new poster in the window caught her eye. Alaska. Everything in that picture was blue and green, with snow on top. And nothing about that landscape was flat. And she fell in love right then and there. Sam must have stared for ten minutes because Bobbie Jo Hudson came out and asked if there was something she could help her with. And Sam just blurted out that it sure would be great to see Alaska some day, and Bobbie Jo laughed and said, "Well, a ticket to get you there would cost almost *four hundred* dollars." That's how she said it: *four hundred* in a big italicized voice. It was pretty clear that she'd never sold a ticket that pricey before, and as Sam thought about it on her way to the library she kind of wondered how on earth anyone made a living out of a travel agency in this town anyway. Nobody ever went anywhere.

She turned in Kathleen Woodiwiss and found herself wandering to the Jack London novels and before she knew it she was back in her room at home, blazing her way through *The Call of the Wild*.

Scraping up every cent she could, including her birthday money and busting open her childhood piggy bank, she took the bus to Seattle, a long series of boat ferries (now that's an amazing thing to a Texas kid), and eventually found her way to the employment office for the new pipeline they were building. When asked what her job skills were she couldn't think of a single thing so she blurted out that she could bake brownies and grill hamburgers and she made a heck of an ice cream sundae. And that got her a job as a camp cook.

Sam made more money than she could have ever

dreamed of, and she met a blue-eyed charmer named Jake Calendar. By that October, when it became obvious that it was going to stay nighttime for the next five months and when she got her fill of trudging out in the snowy dark of the line camp to puke into a latrine every morning, Sam decided that another change was in order. She never told Jake about the baby that would arrive the next summer. She just took the company shuttle to Anchorage and spent a little of her earnings on a plane ticket. She still couldn't face the idea of heading back to flat, Baptist Texas so she landed in Denver. Longer days, but not a whole lot warmer. She bought a used Jeep and headed south, determined not to let the mountains out of her sight. When she landed in Taos, New Mexico, she stopped.

Kelly arrived on a beautiful May morning and it was scary to see that the child had the same brilliant blue eyes, curly brown hair and charm-you-out-of-anything ways as her father.

Those blue eyes fixed on Sam now, as she walked into the kitchen.

"Mom! Hi! Surprise!"

"Kelly. What are you doing here?"

She'd made herself right at home. Dishes were piled in the sink, smeared in red sauce from the spaghetti Sam had left in the fridge a few days earlier. Through the door to the hall, she saw a large black suitcase on the bed in the guest room. A guest room now. At one time it was Kelly's and she still obviously felt entitled.

"You look great, Mom. Have you lost weight?"

Hardly. But that's the kind of charmer Kelly was. She had an amazing ability to ignore criticism and just plow forward with a sunny outlook and a batch of compliments.

That cheery disposition got them through her teen years without a death in the house.

Sam plopped her pack on the counter and washed her hands at the sink.

"What time did you get in?" she asked. "You should have told me you were coming. I would have made dinner."

"Oh that's okay," Kelly said. "I found something." As an afterthought she asked if Sam had eaten anything and offered to warm the rest of the pasta. The tea kettle was hot and so Sam pulled mugs from the cabinet and dunked teabags for both of them.

"So, you got a few days off?" she asked, once they were settled at the table.

"Well, that's the thing."

I'm in trouble, Sam thought. "What 'thing'?"

"You know how I've been stressing over Deborah lately."

Kelly's supervisor truly did sound like the office witch at the mid-sized corporation where she'd been working her way up the ladder.

"This week was the pits. She's been on my ass for two weeks, but it got to be more than her usual PMS or whatever. She has it in for me, Mom. I can't handle her anymore."

They'd had this discussion by phone quite a few times. Kelly swore she'd discussed Deborah's behavior with company management, that everyone else in the department agreed with her, but that nothing ever changed. Sam had been sympathetic but was getting the uneasy feeling that tea and sympathy wasn't what Kelly was after now.

"I've quit," she said.

"Quit? A seventy-thousand a year job, and you've just quit?"

"It's not like there aren't better jobs, Mom. I'm getting my résumé out there."

How many places could have possibly received her résumé since, what, Friday? All sorts of thoughts went through Sam's head—mainly, how was Kelly going to pay back the cash she taken. Unemployment money wasn't an option if she'd just walked out. And there certainly wouldn't be any golden parachute.

Kelly got up and went to the cookie jar, helping herself to the last of the butter cookies. "Don't stress over this, Mom. Something great is going to come through."

Sam rinsed her mug and put the dirty dishes into the dishwasher, refusing to guess at why Kelly left Los Angeles on a moment's notice, or to dwell on the fact that she'd never find a job of that caliber here in Taos.

"I'm tired," Sam said. "We'll talk about this tomorrow."

She closed her bedroom door and put on her nightshirt. A quick call to Beau to let him know there was no emergency and that they could talk more tomorrow. From the living room a reality show began blaring on television. The smell of microwave popcorn drifted through the house. This was too much like the last time Kelly'd shown up, right after her college graduation. Sam pulled the pillow over her head and tried not to think.

Chapter 14

Sam woke early, with an uneasy mix of images running through her head. Beau's kiss last night came back to her, creating an ache inside. Then she remembered that Kelly was in the next room and suspected that she'd only heard half the story about her quick exit from L.A. and her job.

The phone was ringing in the kitchen when she stepped out of the shower. When it became apparent that Kelly wasn't going to get herself out of bed to answer it Sam threw on a robe and dashed for it. A female voice was leaving a message about a cake. She grabbed up the receiver before the answering machine cut off. At this moment, any business was good business.

"I know this is short notice, but is there any way you could do a wedding cake by Thursday?" the female voice inquired, once she realized she was speaking to a real person.

Sam got the details on size and colors and quoted a price, with a little added premium for the fact that she would once again have to drive to Santa Fe for delivery. Sam's own inclination, if she were the customer, would have been to look for the nearest local bakery but as the baker she was more than happy to accept an order. It wasn't as if she were swamped with extra business right now. If Sweet's Sweets was ever going to get off the ground Sam had to jump through a few hoops to get that necessary can-do reputation.

The minute she hung up she made a quick inventory of supplies and calculated a schedule. The three cakes for the tiers would have to be baked the night before assembly and delivery. But she could get busy on the flowers and trim pieces right away. She whipped up a batch of buttercream frosting, tinted part of it in the bride's chosen mauve and started making roses and buds. A darker tint for some of the flowers would add dimension. Even with a traditional cake like this customer wanted, Sam liked to add special touches. She'd no sooner slipped the baking sheet full of roses, on their small paper squares, into the fridge than Beau called.

"How did it go last night?" he asked.

"Same song, next verse. I don't think I'm getting the whole story." She glanced toward Kelly's room. The door remained closed. Some job hunt.

"Thought you might be interested in knowing that some kind of plant toxin showed up in Riley Anderson—uh, Pierre Cantone's system. The M.I. said there was fluid in the lungs, maybe pneumonia, so I don't know if the two are related."

"Odd. Maybe he was having an allergic reaction to something and that caused the fluid." Sam realized that she was merely making wild guesses. "I'm still wondering where the roommate went, too. How weird is it that he just vanished. Do you think someone might have harmed him?"

"No real evidence of that. Maybe with Cantone's death, he simply had no reason to stick around."

That was certainly possible.

"Sam . . . I'd really like to see you again." His voice held that familiar ache.

She glanced again at Kelly's closed door and lowered her voice. "Me too. But it's awkward right now. Your place?"

"Well, that's awkward too. My mother is here."

He'd mentioned his mother before. "Visiting?" she asked, daring to hope.

"No, and that's the thing. She's getting fragile and I've been debating what to do. Nursing homes are just so depressing."

Sam could only imagine. Her own parents were still going pretty strong, and her sister Rayleen lived less than ten miles from them. Whenever Sam talked to friends who were dealing with the elderly and frail, it made her appreciate her situation.

They ended the call without really making any plans.

She was brooding over it when the phone rang again. Delbert Crow. He had another house for her to take care of, this one between town and the Taos Ski Valley. Not exactly a convenient drive, but hey, income was income. She wrote down the details and asked whether there was a key or if she'd need to break in. She knew what the answer would be. Luckily, her tool box was still out in the truck. She told him she could get on it that afternoon.

With another glare at Kelly's closed bedroom door, Sam made herself a sandwich for lunch, knowing she still had to talk to her daughter about repaying the money. Dreading it.

Sam went out to her truck to be sure her tools and lawn equipment were loaded. She doubted that a property on the ski basin road would have an actual, formal lawn but she never knew. Best to be prepared.

Back in the kitchen she grabbed an apple and chips to go with her sandwich and noticed that Kelly's bedroom door stood halfway open. A flush from the bathroom, and she meandered out wearing an oversize T-shirt and loose silk kimono.

"Morning, Mom," she said with a yawn, coming into the kitchen and touching the side of the coffee carafe to see if it was warm.

"It's nearly noon," Sam said. "Coffee went cold hours ago."

Kelly hmmm'd and filled a mug with the cold leftover brew, sticking it into the microwave.

"I've got a property to attend to this afternoon. Do not get into those roses in the fridge. They're for a customer." One of Kelly's favorite things as a teen had been to pop a whole frosting rose into her mouth and just let it melt. "What are your plans today?"

She shot Sam a look that said she'd hoped not to do anything at all.

"We need to talk. Later." Sam gathered her pack and left.

She reached the ski valley property quickly enough. Posted the requisite signage that USDA provides, notifying the world that the property was now under their jurisdiction. The place was high enough in elevation to be largely covered in trees, mostly piñon but with a few taller pines as well. Aside from a summer's worth of mountain wildflowers and grasses to be leveled with the weed trimmer, the outdoor work would be minimal.

The house was a charmer, a picturesque log cabin with a wide porch across the front and a large redwood deck at the back. Wooden planters once held lush annuals, but crisp brown stalks provided the only evidence of them now. Overall, the place was well maintained and Sam wondered what had caused the owner to abandon it.

Inside, it was clear that they'd taken their time moving out. No furniture remained, the kitchen was neat, the refrigerator empty. Utilities had been cut off, apparently, but she checked the breakers anyway and made sure the hot water heater was shut off. This place wouldn't need much at all in the way of cleanup, just some routine maintenance to keep it in showable condition until it sold. She guessed that a sale would come along soon—the property had that kind of curb appeal.

She spent an hour or so inside, sweeping up the few bits of mouse evidence and swiping at some corner cobwebs with a duster, draining the pipes and pouring a little antifreeze into each drain. With freezing temperatures approaching in the next month or so, and no heat in the cabin, frozen pipes would be the biggest potential problem. That done, she replaced the locks and turned her attention to the outdoors.

A split-rail fence surrounded an area that was probably two or three acres. Of that, most had been left natural with just a perimeter of twenty feet or so immediately around the house trimmed, either for appearance or as a firebreak. Sam cranked up her gas weed trimmer and set to work on it, concentrating on the drive and walkways first. The drone of the engine and monotony of cutting neat swathes gave her peace from dwelling on her daughter's messed-up situation. Instead, she found herself thinking of the artist Cantone, imagining that he might have found inspiration in an idyllic mountain setting like this.

The sun had gone behind the surrounding mountains by the time she finished, darkening the property and narrow lane with shade. She packed up her gear, rechecked the locks and headed out.

As long as she was at this end of town, Sam decided she might as well dash by the Cantone property and give things there a quick checkover. It wasn't more than ten minutes out of the way and there was still daylight once she got away from the steep hills surrounding the ski valley.

She zipped along the county road, enjoying the fact that she was out of the house, doing something on her own for a few extra minutes. Betty McDonald's car was in her driveway, Sam noted as she turned in at Cantone's. Some weeds were sprouting along the driveway but otherwise the property looked fairly neat.

Inside, nothing had changed. The smell of drywall mud from her little patch job gave the house an air of freshness, like new construction. In the kitchen she found herself staring at the places where she'd previously seen the greenish haze, but it was harder to spot this time. A faint dusting, barely noticeable now. She still wondered about that, whether she should mention it to Beau.

She locked the front door and turned toward the truck. Beside the driveway were some short plants that she'd never noticed before. They had an odd color, similar to the unusual green she'd spotted inside. On a whim, she walked over and plucked a stem from one. Handling the stem, some of the same substance came off on her fingers. It looked identical.

That probably explained it. Maybe the plant was something Cantone used to mix his paints. Or maybe it was edible and they cooked with it. She found an old sack on the back seat of the truck and carefully wrapped a few stems of the plant in it. She would ask Zoe, her friendly plant expert.

At the Y intersection at the north end of town she happened to glance down at her cell phone on the seat beside her. She'd missed a call, probably while she was behind the hills all afternoon. She recognized Rupert's number and dialed him.

"What's up?" she asked.

"Interesting news flash in the art world." He paused, obviously waiting for her to beg to hear it. She obliged. "Two Cantone paintings have just showed up at an auction house in New York. I inquired, through Esteban, and word is that they came through an artist rep in Santa Fe."

"What, like an agent?"

"No, I think this is more like a broker, someone who finds art from various sources—sometimes artists or their estates, sometimes owners who want to sell a piece. The rep contacts the big auction houses if the piece might bring a higher price at a national or international sale. The two Cantone paintings are some of his earlier work and are considered very rare. They haven't been seen publicly in years."

"Rare, meaning how much in dollars?"

"Well over a million."

Sam's breath caught. How could a man who'd created such valuable art live and die in near poverty? When the sale of one painting would have set him up for life, why hadn't he been able to pay a mortgage on a tiny scrap of property?

"I wonder how and where this art rep got hold of the paintings," she mused.

"No idea. But we can check her out. It's Carolyn Hildebrandt and she's got an office in Santa Fe. I'll call, see what I can learn."

"Give it a try," Sam said. "I'm on my way home. Let me know what you find out."

She stopped at the market for a roasted chicken and a couple of deli salads for dinner, then headed home. She found Kelly stretched out on the couch in sweats, with the TV blaring some kind of reality-show contest between teams of twenty-somethings who couldn't stop jumping up and down and screaming "ohmygod!!!".

"Hey," Sam called out. "I brought dinner."

Kelly shuffled into the kitchen, not bothering to lower the television volume.

"Yumm . . . you remembered my favorite chicken. Thanks, Mom." She helped herself to a heaping plate and started back to the living room.

"Let's eat in here," Sam said. "Get the chance to catch up on things."

She complied but didn't look thrilled about it.

First things first, Sam reminded Kelly that she needed her debit card back and expected her to repay the money she'd taken from the account.

"That wasn't meant to be an open-ended cash supply,

you know. I gave you the card to help with Christmas expenses only, you know."

Kelly had the good grace to hang her head, just a little. Then came the charm. "I know, Mom, and I'm really so grateful for that. I didn't mean to get so far behind on my credit cards. It won't happen again."

"Get the card for me now," Sam said with the biggest smile she could muster. Two could play at this charm game.

Kelly left her dinner plate long enough to retrieve her purse from the bedroom and hand her mother the card. Sam slipped it into her jeans pocket.

"So, what's going to happen now?" Sam asked. "Job, house in L.A., all that?"

Kelly took a deep breath and pushed her plate away. "Well, it's like this. I have no reason to go back to California."

Sam pushed her own plate aside now and gave her daughter a hard stare.

"Real estate has tanked. My house is under water."

Sam envisioned some kind of flood, but she went on.

"It's worth less than I owe on it. I can't refinance because the lenders would never take the loss. I can't sell it because I'd have to come up with two hundred grand to make up the difference. I know I bought too much house at too high a price. Don't even remind me of that." She wouldn't look straight at Sam. "Even if I'd kept my job I was sinking farther behind every month. It was just a matter of time. So I walked away. Everybody's doing it."

Sam wanted to launch into the whole motherly lecture about what if everybody were jumping off the cliff, but that sounded way too much like what her own mother would have said.

"Everybody? Kell, really?"

"Okay, not *every*body." She carried the dishes to the sink and dumped the remains of the uneaten food. "Mom, I tried. I really did. I've been looking for a new job for months. There's nothing." Unshed tears made her voice go ragged.

Sam could have gone into the whole 'then why did you leave the job you had' speech but that, too, was what her mother would have said. She let the silence fill the room.

"I'll find something. I know I will. But I need to stay here awhile. It won't be long."

What choice did she have? Give up her privacy and put her hot new boyfriend on hold. Okay, so that versus a homeless daughter—Sam knew she'd let her stay.

"One month. I want you online every day, looking and putting in applications." What was she saying? That she'd kick her out in thirty days if she hadn't moved on? Yes.

Easy to say, but what would she really *do*?

She walked into the living room and switched off the TV and pointed Kelly to her computer on the desk in the corner. Job applications were no longer a nine-to-five proposition.

While Kelly pecked away at the keys Sam showered and changed into soft flannel pj's. She got out her calendar and marked check-back dates for each of her properties. She would need to keep the yards maintained until winter set in, plus go back to each and make sure they were tidy and mouse-free until they sold. The cabin she'd visited today would require snow removal by December, and she would have to contract that out to someone else. Most places sold within a month or two, but even their small rural counties weren't immune to the real estate problems that were hitting other parts of the country. Sam might have more long-term jobs than she'd reckoned on.

Kelly was still happily tapping away at the computer keys so Sam took a moment to call Beau and fill him in on the situation, given that she'd left him pretty bewildered last night. Once she'd covered her daughter's circumstances, she remembered the earlier call.

"Rupert told me today that two Cantone paintings came up for auction in New York," she told him. "Remember those blank spots and the nails on the walls in his house? I have the strangest feeling that millions of dollars in art might have been hanging in that little place at one time."

His question was the same as hers—why hadn't Cantone sold something and afforded himself a better lifestyle.

"Maybe he just wanted a simple life," she said. "Nothing wrong with that. But I still get a weird feeling about that situation, the guy who was living with him. It would have been so easy for some unscrupulous bum to take advantage of the artist, maybe even kill him."

"Murder by pneumonia?" he said. "It wouldn't be the most efficient way to off someone."

"Still—I wonder where the other guy went. You know, it's entirely possible that someone else came along—someone who knew the value of the art—and maybe the roommate was also a victim of foul play." She remembered Betty McDonald's gossip about neighbors who didn't like Cantone. When she mentioned it to Beau he said there hadn't been time for him to get out there and question anyone else. Other cases were beginning to take precedence.

"Sam, we don't know that Cantone was a victim of anything. Probably he was old and simply got sick and died."

Still, she just couldn't let go of the idea that the

roommate was out there somewhere, dead or alive. She realized that Kelly's attention seemed to have wandered toward her conversation. She lowered her voice to say goodbye to Beau. As soon as she clicked off the call she turned to her daughter

"Any luck?"

Kelly quickly turned back to the screen. "Mom, it doesn't quite work that way."

Sam paced the kitchen for a minute but doing nothing wasn't her style. Remembering that the Chocoholics Unanimous group would be meeting again tomorrow, she whipped up a batch of brownies and called Ivan at the bookstore to confirm that she could deliver them in the morning. Then, knowing that Rupert was a night owl, she phoned him to see if he'd learned anything new about the origin of those paintings.

"Well."

Another of his long stories. She checked the timer on the oven and sat down.

"I called the art rep at her office. Then I got to thinking, what was I going to say? Just blurt it out that we knew where Cantone had been living and demand to know where she got the man's art? No. I remembered how I handled something like that when I wrote *The Jewel Heist*—you remember those few mysteries I did?—how it's always better to confront someone in person rather than over the phone."

Sam found herself twirling her hand in mid-air, as if that would hurry him up.

"So I told the lady that I represent a wealthy woman who is interested in Cantone's work, and I set up an appointment for tomorrow."

"What wealthy woman?"

"You, my dear. You will be the wealthy client, and that will get us into her office."

Sam howled out loud. Kelly stared at her through the doorway.

"Rupert, how on earth am I going to convince this lady who works with wealthy clients all the time that I'm one of them? There's not a thing in my closet that came from better than JC Penney."

He hmmm'd for a second. "I'll work on that. I probably have something I can loan you. If all else fails, we'll go for the grunge look."

Uh-huh. Me in grunge, she thought. *About as likely as me in Versace.*

He said he'd be over in the morning and they'd take it from there.

Chapter 15

Sam had to admit that she didn't sleep a lot that night. She had one nightmare in which she was about ninety and Kelly, in her seventies, was trying to convince her that she should go into a nursing home. Kelly still occupied the spare bedroom in Sam's house and by the look of it hadn't left in forty years. She woke from that one in a sweat.

Then she began obsessing over how she'd ever pull off Rupert's little deception with the art dealer. An actress, she was not. There was simply no way he could pack her chunky body into anything designer. Her brain raced through the contents of her closet, the supply of jeans, stretch pants and work shirts, with the nicest thing she owned being a black crepe dress she'd bought for a funeral three or four years ago. And shoes—forget that. She owned three pair of sneakers, the black patent leather pumps to go with the black dress, and some Birkenstock knock-offs from Wal-Mart. Surely Rupert was fashion savvy enough to know that he'd never seen her wearing anything that could remotely fit the role.

By three a.m. she'd slid into delirium, considering whether the costume shops would be open this far in advance of Halloween. By five, she gave up on sleep and got up. A lengthy reconnoiter of her closet revealed exactly what she already knew. Nothing.

She brewed some coffee, then went into the bathroom and studied the mirror. This idea was becoming laughable. That face had too many bags and pouches, not to mention years of sunshine without benefit of weekly facials. Any fool could see that no spa had ever spent a day on this wreck. Sam had nearly sunk into despair when Rupert appeared at her back door at eight.

"Rupe, I . . ."

"Not to fear, dear lady. I thought about this all night."

Please let him say he's changed his mind, she silently begged. We're backing out of this idiotic scheme.

He held up a garment bag. "I have *the* perfect thing."

He bustled into her bedroom, tossed the bag on the bed and unzipped it. "Now, as I recall, you have a nice little basic black dress."

How would he remember that? Gay men and fashion sense, she supposed. She pulled it from the closet, checking the tag to be sure it wasn't left over from two sizes ago.

"Put it on," he prompted.

He busied himself with the contents of the garment bag while Sam shed her robe and stepped into the dress.

"Now, to top it off . . ." He held up a jacket in vivid

turquoise silk, sewn in concentric panels so that the nap created a sunrise effect. She slipped her arms into it and discovered that it fit perfectly.

"It was a little small on me," he said. He noticed her expression. "Hey, I had to describe it accurately when I wrote Helena Deveau wearing it in *Passion's Glory*. The rogue, Max Everhard, cast it into the river right before he took her, there in the forest."

Sam hadn't read that one, and suddenly was glad of that omission. He cleared his throat and turned back to the bag. From a small silk pouch he produced a white gold Patek Philippe watch with diamonds lining the face (another research expense?) and a tasteful string of pearls.

"Rupe, this must have cost thousands!"

"Twenty-five seven. Put it on."

Yikes, what if something happened to the thing. Sam double-checked the clasp.

"The shoes," he announced. "I seem to remember that you wear a nine."

"How do you—?" Never mind. She rummaged in a drawer and came up with hosiery in a new package. No way were her legs in shape to go bare. She re-checked the expensive watch clasp and put her plain-jane digital one into her new jewelry box.

"What time are we meeting this woman?" Sam sat at her dresser, stroking the lumpy surface of the box. It warmed her chilled fingers.

He stared at the back of his wrist. "In fifteen minutes. Not to worry, my dear. The wealthy are always fashionably late. If we're there by ten she won't worry. In fact, let her worry. She thinks we're going to spend a shitload of money this morning."

"So I have time to drop off a platter of brownies at the bookstore?"

"Absolutely. Now let's decide about your makeup." He walked over to stand behind Sam and looked at her face in the mirror. "Girl, I don't know what you've been doing but your skin is absolutely radiant. Is that new deputy sheriff making your eyes sparkle like that?"

"No. there is no *sparkle* between us." She blushed when he caught the fib in the mirror.

She didn't want to admit that she'd scarcely thought of Beau in the last twelve hours, with everything else on her mind. And she certainly didn't tell Rupert that only an hour ago she'd felt hopeless over her looks. He was right. The woman staring back at her now was a younger, slimmer version of herself. Glowing. He picked up her hairbrush and with a couple of deft flips, got the shaggy strands to behave perfectly.

Sam stared at the little wooden box and swore that the colored stones were more brilliant than she'd ever seen them.

They finally got away from Taos at nine-fifteen, Rupert driving them in his Land Rover. Ivan, at Mysterious Happenings, had stared at Sam, clearly unsure what to make of the changes. She brushed it off by saying that they were on their way to a masquerade. He knew Rupert well enough that he probably believed it.

By the time they waltzed into Carolyn Hildebrant's small gallery at eleven o'clock, Rupert had coached Sam sufficiently to set her nerves to rest—let him do most of the talking; if Hildebrandt wanted Sam's opinion on anything, just say 'it's a very interesting piece' or 'I'm considering it.'

"Mrs. Knightly," the art rep gushed.

Knightly? Where did—? Sam glanced at Rupert who gave a tiny shrug. What else had he left out of his briefing? She smiled coolly at Hildebrandt, as she imagined someone named Mrs. Knightly would do.

"I understand you are interested in the work of Pierre Cantone," Hildebrandt said, leading them to a secondary room where she offered tea and some exquisitely decorated cookies. Sam looked them over and swiped a couple of decorating ideas from them.

The room was a combination of a private viewing space and study. Deep leather wing chairs faced a wall where one painting at a time could be displayed. Whatever currently hung there was covered at the moment by drapes. Shelves lined one wall, filled with books on art, botany and nature, along with small but pricey objects. One statue of a sleek cat polished to a gleaming black finish caught Sam's eye.

". . . such a shock, wasn't it?" She realized that Ms. Hildebrandt had asked her a question. Somehow, she didn't think 'interesting' or 'considering' were the right answer.

Rupert stepped in. "Yes, the art world lost a great man with the passing of Cantone."

Sam nodded, turning her mouth downward and biting her lip a little.

"Of course, his work immediately tripled in value," Hildebrandt said. "We've placed two pieces with Sotheby's and another privately, just in the last week."

Quick work. Sam wondered exactly when Carolyn Hildebrandt had become aware of Cantone's demise. Certainly before the discovery of the grave last Tuesday.

"I wasn't aware that there were any Cantones that

weren't already in private hands," Rupert said. "I wonder who is offering theirs for sale."

"Well, of course I can't give details. But there are family members."

Sam soaked all this up while feigning interest in another piece on the shelves, a crystal globe with a miniature flower garden of glass inside. Family members. Rupert had uncovered only the one sister.

"Ah, Sophie's young son," Rupert said, with just the right amount of sorrow in his voice. If she hadn't known better, Sam might have believed that he was best of friends with the mother and her offspring. Hildebrandt fell for it.

"Yes. Hobart. I understand that was a family name on the Killington side of the family."

"It was," Rupert said. His acting was better than Sam ever imagined. "What's Bart up to these days?"

"Actually, he's recently moved here to Santa Fe. He'll be stopping by here later."

"And he is the seller."

A slight nod. "Well, I know you must be eager to see the piece." Ms. Hildebrandt stepped to the side and pulled a hidden cord. The drapes slid back to reveal a painting about eighteen inches wide, framed in a dark wood that brought out the deep colors in the pastoral scene. Sam immediately recognized the style.

Rupert actually gasped. He recovered quickly, though. "They never fail to impress, do they?"

Hildebrandt looked at Sam.

"Interesting piece."

Rupert gave her a look. Maybe she should have gushed a little more, but she *was* following his coaching.

"You have an excellent eye," Carolyn Hildebrandt said.

"It truly is one of Cantone's more interesting pieces." She walked over to it and Sam sent Rupert a 'ha-ha' look behind her back. "Note the use of cadmium red right here. No other artist of his time would have thought of such a move. It just pulls the eye to that particular section of the tree, doesn't it?"

"Brilliant," Sam said, picking up a new word for her art vocabulary.

The art dealer smiled at her. "It truly was a brilliant move on his part. The very thing that turned Cantone into a legend."

Sam nodded as if she had a clue.

"This piece will go to New York on Thursday unless I have a buyer for it here in New Mexico."

Sam stared at the painting for what seemed like the right amount of time. "I'm considering it. Very seriously."

Rupert stepped in. "Mrs. Knightly is only in town on business for two days. We'll have a decision for you soon."

He turned to Sam. "My dear, shall we?"

She took his arm and nodded to the dealer. Out on the sidewalk he raised her fingertips and kissed them. "Well done, Sam."

They walked to the lot where he'd parked and it was all she could do not to kick up her heels. She'd pulled off her first acting job.

"So, we know we're looking for Hobart Killington, but I'm guessing he's not going to have a listed phone number," she said, once they'd settled into the car.

"True, but did you catch Carolyn's comment that Bart would be coming to the gallery this afternoon?"

"But she clearly didn't intend that we meet Hobart, and

we don't even know what he looks like."

He pulled a laptop computer from the backseat. "We will pretty soon."

They parked outside a café that boasted free wi-fi and within five minutes had found a web page for one of the major auction houses, recently updated with a photo showing the nephew who had re-introduced the great Cantone's work to the world. Bart Killington could pass for any age from twenty to forty. Based on her previous research Sam guessed that he must be in his mid-thirties. A high forehead, dark brows, thin face with a prominent nose. He wore his dark hair combed straight back, a trim dark goatee, a tuxedo.

"The only problem is, talking to him without the nosy art dealer right there," Rupert said.

Sam had been thinking about what to say when they got the chance to speak with the nephew. And the more she thought about it, the more she wanted to see him in his element, at home. She had some suspicions that needed to be confirmed.

Chapter 16

Sam was getting hungry and the whole Mrs. Knightly outfit was beginning to make her itch—she didn't do dresses very often. Luckily, she'd thought of that and brought a change of clothes. She suggested to Rupert that they go inside the café for some lunch. While he ordered her a Reuben sandwich she slipped into the ladies room where she traded the dress and silk jacket for jeans and a soft pullover from her roomy shoulder bag.

"Better," she told him when she came back to the table. "I'm glad I could fool Carolyn Hildebrandt with the Mrs. Knightly getup, but it's better that I talk to Bart Killington as myself."

They devoured their sandwiches and headed back toward Hildebrandt's gallery. Parking was at a premium on the narrow street but they found a spot that gave a decent view of the front door from about a half-block away. Then came the wait. They had no idea what time Bart would be coming, provided he didn't change his mind and not show at all. Two hours dragged by.

"What if he came and went while we were eating?" Sam said.

"Patience, my dear. The lady said he was coming this afternoon. We were back here at twelve-thirty, so the odds are in our favor."

Sam wasn't very tolerant with this kind of thing, but resisted twitching in her seat. There were so many other things she could be doing this afternoon—checking on her properties, pre-making more decorations for that wedding cake, nagging her daughter about getting a job.

To amuse herself she pulled an old receipt out of her bag, smoothed the eight-and-a-half by eleven page, and began sketching ideas for her pastry shop on the back. Someday Sweet's Sweets would become a reality, not merely a sideline business run from a cramped kitchen, represented by a name on a business card.

"Sam, look up. I think that's him," Rupert said.

The dark-haired man was a block away, walking toward them, on the shady side of the street. Just before he reached the gallery he passed through a shaft of sunlight and Sam got a clear look.

"You're right." They both sat straighter in their seats.

Bart stayed inside for nearly thirty minutes and Sam was starting to get impatient again but Rupert told her stories from some of his more memorable book signings to keep her from jumping out of the car and invading the gallery. Before he got to the one about the male cover model and the romance writers convention of 2004, Sam spotted Bart on the sidewalk.

"There he is—be ready!"

He cranked up the Land Rover and started a slow maneuver out of the tight parking spot. Bart got into a dark green Jaguar with the dealer sticker still on it.

"Don't let him see us," she said.

"Honey, I've written enough stalker scenes to know how to handle it."

She had no choice but to believe him. They stayed back a few car lengths but she still worried that only a blind guy wouldn't notice the hulking SUV.

Apparently Bart didn't. He drove through the city without making any sort of evasive moves. By the time they got on Highway 285 northbound, she began to wonder just how far away he really lived. But then he exited near the opera and wound his way through one of those exclusive neighborhoods where each house has its own little hilltop, some game of king-of-the-mountain, Santa Fe style. At least the Land Rover wasn't out of place here, as Sam's big red pickup truck might have been.

Rupert did a good job of maneuvering—staying just one curve behind the Jag, but catching up in time that they didn't lose him on an obscure lane or something. When the Jag slowed she realized he was about to turn in at a driveway on the right. Rupert let the SUV coast nearly to a stop until the car began the climb up the steep drive. A territorial style adobe sat at the top of the rise, a massive thing with a few gables and some stained glass thrown in for good measure.

Sam hadn't thought about what their actual approach would be. Rupert handled it by bringing the Land Rover up to the driveway entrance and simply letting it coast to a stop.

By the time Bart was out of his car in front of the huge house, Rupert had slammed his door, stalked to the front of his vehicle and raised the hood.

"Damn it all!" he shouted.

Bart fell for it. He came to the top of the drive, peering curiously down at the stalled vehicle.

Sam got out and joined Rupert at the front of his car. He pulled out a cell phone, flipped it open and then made a gesture of disgust and jammed it back into his pocket. "Follow my lead," he said through clenched teeth.

Pretending to have just noticed his surroundings he glanced up the driveway and feigned surprise at seeing Bart standing there.

Maybe Rupert should have stayed with the theater.

Sam stood there like she didn't have a clue what to do, which wasn't far off the mark.

"Oh, say—" Rupert began walking up the driveway and she followed along. "Might we borrow your telephone? My cell seems to be dead."

With the big SUV blocking his driveway, Bart didn't have much choice. Rupert kept up the chat as they crossed a wide circular drive. "I just don't know about these maintenance shops anymore. Just had the thing worked on. Here we are, down from Taos for the day, supposed to have tea with the Rutledges—" He waved vaguely up the road.

"Sure, no problem," Bart said. "Come on in."

Piles of dirt and several large landscaping boulders sat beside the driveway and nearby front entry.

"Pardon the mess," he said. "I've just moved in and there's a ton of stuff to do."

He opened the heavy, carved front door and ushered them inside. Pride of new ownership was evident. He couldn't resist pointing out a few features of the home as he showed them into the kitchen (which Sam would have killed for), all granite tops and stainless appliances.

Rupert made a show of punching in some numbers and demanding to speak to the service manager. Sam sent a weak smile toward Bart.

"Samantha Sweet. Sorry, we should have introduced ourselves sooner. My friend is Rupert Penrick." She glanced through an archway into a dining room. "Oh my, is that a Cantone?"

She walked toward it without exactly waiting for Bart to offer.

"We heard that Cantone recently passed away. In Taos. The whole town is in shock."

From the kitchen Rupert called out. "What's your number, Mr . . .?"

"Killington." He rattled off the number without a pause.

How naïve was this guy? Inviting total strangers in and then giving his number?

Before he had the chance to realize his blunder, Sam pulled at his arm. "Is that *another* one?" She pointed to a second framed painting on the opposite wall.

"Rupert, you won't believe this," she said as he came walking in from the kitchen, muttering about how the shop would need to call him back in a few minutes.

"Mr. Killington has two of Cantone's paintings. I was just telling him . . ."

Rupert reached out and touched her arm. "Sam, hold it. Killington? Are you— No, couldn't be. Sophie Cantone— Killington's son? You are Cantone's nephew?"

They couldn't flat-out interrogate the guy, but there

were other ways to get information.

"But we heard— Didn't you live near Taos with your uncle?" Sam turned to Rupert. "Isn't that what we heard? That the artist had a nephew caring for him?"

Bart looked a little uncomfortable but apparently she'd given him the opening he needed.

"I actually had lost contact with my uncle for a number of years. The whole family had. After Mother died, I didn't quite know where to turn. Then I discovered where he was."

"In that tiny house, practically living in poverty." She shook her head sadly.

"Well, uh, yes."

"And you offered to bring him here, to your beautiful home?"

"Uh, actually, I hadn't found this place yet. I wanted to take him in, to have him come to my place in California, but he was just too ill to travel. And he didn't want to leave New Mexico. He always loved it here. All I could do was to move in with him and care for him, in his own house."

Uh-huh.

But before she could ask any more questions, Rupert's cell phone rang. He jumped.

"Oh my, I guess I have a signal again."

Chapter 17

Rupert took the call, stepping into the kitchen for privacy. While he um-hmm'd a couple of times, Sam turned back to Bart.

"You know, the Sheriff in Taos County had a lot of questions about Mr. Cantone's death. It looked like a lot of art was missing from the house." Those blank spots—nails without pictures—had been bothering her from day one. "And the fact that he was buried in the back yard in a practically unmarked grave . . ."

"Look, I don't know who you are and I don't especially care what some small town sheriff thinks. I am Pierre Cantone's sole heir. He was buried according to his wishes and his will left me everything."

"And you went from living in the spare room in a house that was barely more than a shack, to . . . this. All in just a few months' time?"

Bart's tone became defensive. "I sold one painting. It

went quickly because no new Cantone works had appeared on the market in years. So, yes, I bought myself a nicer lifestyle with the proceeds. I have nothing to apologize for."

A tap on the shoulder got her attention. "Sweetie," Rupert said. "I think we can be on our way. The service manager suggested something I might try, to get the car started." He glanced at Bart. "If it doesn't work, they'll send a tow truck. We'll be out of your way shortly."

He took her elbow and steered her out the front door.

"What was that all about?" she said as they walked down the drive. "Did you actually call a service shop?"

"Oh no. I just made that up. It was time to get you out of there." He caught her look. "Honey, what more were you going to learn? And you were just pissing him off."

Well, that was probably true.

"He claims that Cantone left him the entire estate."

"And that might very well be true."

"But then why—?"

"Why did Cantone live in near-squalor? Why did this nephew happen to show up at just the right moment? Honey, I don't think we're ever going to know that."

Sam fumed while Rupert did some little thing under the hood. The Land Rover started right up. Rupert looked up toward the house and gave a little wave to Bart, who stood on the wide front steps.

"I just don't like all the coincidences," she muttered as they drove away.

By the time they got to Taos she'd cooled slightly. She would ask Beau how they might find out about the artist's will. And she would damn sure give him a thorough description of the massive new house, the art on the walls, and—thanks to Rupert's quick thinking—the nephew's phone number.

Wednesday morning Sam hit the floor running. She mixed batter for the wedding cake, and put the first layers in to bake. A pain with a normal home-sized oven—they'd have to be done two at a time until she had enough to form the tiers. She'd had her eye on a good commercial baking oven for a long time, but there was simply no way to adapt her little kitchen for it. While she waited for the timer, she whipped up a batch of royal icing and created lace insets that would dry hard and could then be placed around the sides of the largest tier. She would pipe dots and swirls for the traditional look that the bride wanted.

Kelly wandered out of her room around ten, eyed the production in the kitchen—cakes on cooling racks, trays of lace and roses, the smell of cake baking in the oven—and opted for coffee and a muffin. When asked about the job search, she shrugged and walked away.

Sam resisted the urge to say something more, to make suggestions of places in town where she might apply. Truthfully, it wasn't so much wanting to give motherly advice as it was to nag her daughter until she got her privacy back.

She pulled the final layers from the oven, tucked the decorative elements back into the fridge to harden, and left the cakes to cool thoroughly before she could touch them again. According to her calendar, this was the day to make another run by the Martinez place, and she figured she could work that in before starting the assembly on the cake. She wanted to have it completely decorated today, so it could firm up and be ready for delivery tomorrow.

Bertha Martinez's little place needed some yard work, but Sam wasn't prepared to devote the time today. She swept dry leaves from the porch, then went inside and checked the places she thought of as hot-spots. This time of year, as the nights started to get cold, mice were likely to come looking for food and warm winter beds so she checked their usual favorite haunts—under sinks, in cabinets and pantries. Sometimes the little critters looked for a vulnerable spot in upholstered furniture where they could rip out some padding and make themselves a cozy nest. She found one suspicious little hole in the sofa and couldn't remember if it had been there before. She kept a few packages of yummy poison in the truck, so she set out a few in inconspicuous corners. She'd check them again in a few more days.

She was almost ready to lock up when her cell phone rang and she saw that it was Beau.

"How are things going with Kelly?" he asked. "I notice she's still at your place."

She filled him in on their little talk the other night, Kelly's financial problems and the fact that she'd left her job in a snit. She could tell he was trying hard not to offer advice. She changed the subject by letting him know what she and Rupert had done yesterday.

"Sam . . ."

"I know. It probably wasn't the smartest thing."

"That nephew could have gotten violent with you. You know nothing about him."

"He didn't seem the type. Plus, I had Rupert there."

Beau huffed to let her know how much protection he thought Rupert might provide.

"Anyway, it was uneventful and I got some good information. Bart readily admitted that he'd been living in the house with Cantone and that he'd buried him in the backyard."

"He volunteered that?"

"Well, I asked him. But he didn't deny it. Said it was in accordance with his uncle's wishes." She locked Bertha's front door and walked toward her truck as she talked. "He said his uncle left him everything, including a bunch of paintings."

"Hmm . . . I have a hard time believing there's been time to probate the will and distribute the estate."

"Me too. I don't know how that stuff works."

"I'm not up on all of it either, but I'm fairly certain that he can't just be selling paintings and spending the money. Not until the state gets its hefty share of inheritance taxes. On the other hand, without a death certificate or public burial, until you reported the grave to me the state probably had no knowledge of the death at all."

"And that would be just the way Bart Killington would want it, don't you think? I'm just surprised that he stayed so close by. He could have easily headed back to California or skipped the country."

"He might not have known any better. Just assumed he could take everything and go on his merry way."

"But, Beau, what if there's more? I can't get over the feeling that Cantone was young to die. What if his nephew saw a great opportunity and took it?"

"No one says that criminals don't do dumb things."

"I still have a lot of Cantone's papers. Something told me not to just throw them out. Maybe I'll go through them and see if there's a copy of a will. It would be interesting to know if we're getting the full story from Bart."

"If you do find one, there will probably be an attorney's name with it, or somewhere in his papers. The attorney would be the best one to follow up with. It's outside the jurisdiction of my department unless a judge orders us to serve papers."

"The other thing that's bugging me is the question of reburying Cantone. Now that we know there is a living relative, shouldn't he be involved?"

"Yeah, and I guess I need to check that out and probably pay a visit to him. The property no longer belongs to Cantone, unless Bart wants to step in and pay the mortgage and back taxes." Beau didn't sound happy about getting this involved.

Sam gave him Bart's phone number and drove back home.

Kelly was gone when she got there. A glance into her room showed an unmade bed and an explosion of clothing on every surface. No hints about where she'd gone, but it wasn't back to L.A.

She began the assembly of the wedding cake for tomorrow's delivery—icing each tier in ivory buttercream, then stacking the tiers on dowels with separators between.

While letting the smooth icing set, she dragged out the box of papers she'd brought from Cantone's place. Aside from the bank statements there were really only a couple of folders that looked like they contained anything important. Most were paid bills dating back a year or so. She carefully paged through every sheet but there was no will and nothing with an attorney's name. If there had been a will, as Bart Killington claimed, chances were good that he had the only copy. The knowledge chafed at her.

She washed her hands thoroughly and went back to the

cake. Her favorite part was the actual decorating. She pulled bowls of buttercream that she'd made earlier from the refrigerator and began filling pastry bags. Scrolls and fluted ribbons flowed from the tip of the bag, and her royal-icing lace blended in with the soft frosting beautifully. Two hours slipped by as she became completely immersed in the work. Finally, she took the mauve roses from the fridge and placed them, piping a few leaves around them for authenticity. Tiny pearlized dots completed the look.

Out on the service porch was a separate refrigerator with most of the shelves removed, which she used for cake storage until the actual delivery. She opened the door to it, hefted the forty pounds of cake and ornate frosting, and placed it gently inside. Done. At least for today.

She heard Kelly's car in the driveway as she headed back to the kitchen. Maybe she should threaten to put Kelly to work as her clean-up assistant. That would certainly get her out there pushing harder to find a desk job.

"Hey, Mom," Kelly said, her brown curls bouncing as she came into the kitchen. "Did you see the message I left on the counter?"

Sam looked around but every surface in the kitchen was filled with baking and decorating utensils.

"Near the microwave," Kelly said.

Wedged into the narrow space between the oven and the wall Sam got a glimpse of yellow paper. She picked it out and saw that someone wanted an order of cupcakes for a birthday party tomorrow afternoon. Suddenly, a week with more business than she could handle. When it rains it pours, as her mother used to say. As long as the kitchen was a mess anyway, she might as well get with it now.

She called the customer to verify details—suggested buttercream frosting, since there was a lot of it left—and then mixed up a batch of batter and started baking the two-dozen cupcakes. While they were in the oven she searched out her largest decorating tips. Huge flowers were quick and easy to make with the oversized tips, and she thought they'd go over well with the birthday girl, a thirty-something who'd heard about Sam through her friend Erica. She quickly tinted frosting in a variety of colors and placed it aside in the fridge.

"How about if I make dinner tonight?" Kelly offered, coming in from her room. "I learned a quick pasta dish awhile back, if you've got some small tomatoes and linguine."

Sam took back most of the negative thoughts she'd had about her daughter in the last twenty-four hours. At times she could be so thoughtful. Seeing mom up to her chin in dirty dishes and frosting must have triggered her cooperative-gene. Or not.

"I'm starving!" she said. "Is it okay if I get started on the pasta now?"

Sam filled the dishwasher, dumped the rest of the buttery items into hot water to soak, and gladly turned the kitchen over.

"I'm going to get a quick shower," Sam told her. "When the timer on the oven goes off, just take the cupcakes out and set them on these racks."

When she stepped out of the shower ten minutes later she got the distinctive whiff of smoke.

Chapter 18

Sam snatched up a robe and dashed for the kitchen.

"Kelly! What's burning?"

She emerged from the living room where some female gossip show on TV must have held her attention.

The cupcakes sat on the table, safe on their cooling racks.

"Oh shit—the garlic bread!" Kelly dashed for the oven but it was too late. The blackened bread was too far gone. "Oh no, this would have been so perfect with the pasta."

Sam opened a window and the back door, fanning the air with a towel before the smoky smell could saturate her baked goods.

"It's okay," she said. "We can live without bread."

"Oh, god, I can't believe how stupid I am." Kelly flopped

into a chair at the table, her head in her hands.

"Kell, it's really okay." Sam dumped the burned toast into the trash and aimed a shot of air freshener toward the center of the room. The tomato sauce was simmering gently on the burner and it really did look good. And the pasta seemed nearly ready. "Look, everything else is going to be just perfect."

Kelly raised a tearstained face. "Really?"

"Really." Sam started to pat her on the shoulder but the phone rang just then. She wasn't sure she could handle another last-minute bakery order but it turned out to be Zoe.

"Just the person I wanted to talk to," Sam told her. "I've been wondering if we might trade vehicles again tomorrow. I have a large cake to deliver and I think yours would be more steady than my big old truck." Another expense she'd have to consider, even before opening her shop, would be a better vehicle. A small van was what she really needed.

"Sure, no problem. I'll bring it over now. I was just checking to see if you could use some zucchini from the garden. I've got tons."

Sam readily agreed because she'd just come across a new recipe for zucchini bread and wanted to give it a try. She could tweak it and turn it into a seasonal signature bakery item.

Kelly's pasta dish produced way more than the two of them could possibly eat so she sent Zoe home with enough dinner for herself and Darryl. By the time they sat down to eat Sam was more than ready to be off her feet for awhile.

Darling daughter apparently sensed that her old mom was worn out, so she offered to clean up the kitchen. Sam sat at the table piping huge roses, chrysanthemums, hydrangeas and lilies onto the red-velvet cupcake tops. Simple to do but very showy—she felt sure the customer would be thrilled at having something different than a traditional birthday cake. As she finished with each of the decorating tips she tossed them into a bowl of hot water; Kelly took them to the sink and washed everything thoroughly.

"Mom," she said. "Thanks for taking me in. I really mean that." She paused from wiping the counter tops and fixed Sam with those aquamarine eyes.

Sam teared up and reached out to give her a hug. Despite those frustrating times when she made rash decisions, she still loved the kid.

Kelly went into her room where Sam could see her picking up clothes and hanging them in the closet. What kind of epiphany had she had this afternoon?

She glanced at the clock. It wasn't too late to call Rupert.

He answered on the first ring and said he'd just gotten in from a reception at one of the more popular galleries on the plaza.

"Girl, I tell you, Cantone is all the rage right now."

"Really?"

"It's like a badge of honor for Taos that he was living here. Everyone wants to put together a fund to have a proper funeral for him. People were appalled—I mean, really shocked—that he'd been living in poverty."

"I've wondered about that too. Seeing what the sale of just one painting netted for Bart—that car, the huge house, new furnishings and everything . . . Why didn't Cantone do that? Sell one painting and buy himself a comfortable lifestyle?"

"Well."

Another of Rupert's gossip-fests. Sam went into the living room and snuggled into a corner of the sofa.

"Word is," he paused, building the drama, "that Cantone simply didn't like people. He became more reclusive with each passing year. I mean, no one had seen him at any public function in twenty years or more. The old gala showings were gone. The appearances at theatre opening nights, the charity balls—Cantone simply wrote off all of the social life."

"Was that because of his wife's death?"

"Some of it, probably. But he really shut down in the last ten years, I mean, just disappeared. Well, you know that even *I* had no idea he was living so close to Taos."

"But surely the man needed an income. To allow foreclosure on his home, when he had plenty of assets . . . I just don't get it."

"Again, part of the legend. I've heard that he got so attached to his paintings that he actually threw his one-time manager out—this was years ago—when the man suggested that Cantone sell something. He would not let go of anything."

She thought about that. She'd heard of people who began to hoard as they got older. In fact, she'd been assigned a couple of caretaking properties where she'd actually had to get a roll-off to haul away huge amounts of clutter. But Cantone's house had not been nearly that bad. Apparently his clingy tendencies applied only to his art. And there seemed something more deliberate about Cantone's approach, she thought as she remembered the hidden sketchbook she'd found in the wall.

"Well, Rupert, maybe it's understandable. He was getting older, maybe not producing a lot of new work, so he didn't want to let go of what he had."

He mumbled an acknowledgement.

"Of course, the big gossip tonight was about this nephew who suddenly showed up on the scene," he said. "I mean, no one's heard of this kid and now all at once he's the heir to everything."

Sam thought about what Beau had said about a will and probate and estate taxes, but didn't want to bring it up with Rupert. As much as she loved the guy, he truly was a gossip of the highest order. The legalities of the artist's estate didn't need to become cocktail party prattle.

Besides, she still wanted to find out the truth about the will, and if everyone in the art world began talking about it the odds were good that word would get back to Bart Killington. That might be the very thing to send him south of the border.

They chatted on about nothing in particular for another three minutes, then Rupert said he ought to get back to his latest manuscript, which his editor had returned for some changes. She hung up, still reflecting on the question of Cantone's last will and testament.

Sam's alarm went off way too early the next morning and she groaned at the intrusion. She'd set it because she had far too many things on today's calendar to indulge in her usual leisurely wake-up routine. Much as she felt tempted to hit the snooze button, she didn't. She sat on the edge of the bed and rubbed a little circulation into her face, thinking she was getting too old for this.

Why am I chasing around, she wondered, trying to start

a business, taking jobs that send me running all over the county, and then nosing around to check out the death of a man I didn't know much about less than a week ago?

Resisting the energy-drain of so much analysis, she dragged herself to the bathroom and splashed cold water on her face, which served only to give her a wet face—no magical energizer. Patting dry, she brushed her teeth, gargled the strongest mouthwash in the house, and brushed her hair until it flew straight up in electric spikes. She still didn't feel very awake.

In the kitchen she started the coffee maker, brewing the stuff with an extra scoop of dark roast. The birthday cupcakes sat on the kitchen table, covered with a plastic shell. She rummaged for her invoice book and wrote out a bill for the customer, taping it to the plastic cover so she wouldn't forget it. The short-notice wedding cake also had to go out today.

While the coffee dripped she went back to her room and searched for her black slacks and white blouse, her quasi-uniform when she made deliveries to places like Casa de Tranquilidad. She laid the clothes out on the bed. They needed to stay clean until she was ready to drive to Santa Fe this afternoon.

For the morning, her duties were to get back to Bertha Martinez's place and do some yard trimming. For that, she could get by with jeans and an old shirt. She donned them quickly and returned to the kitchen where she poured a large mug of the strong black brew. Sitting at her dresser, she was rummaging through a drawer in search of sunscreen when she heard a vehicle pull into the driveway.

Beau's cruiser stopped with a slight squeal of brakes.

Oh god, she was in no shape to be seen by a man that

she didn't want to scare away. She set the sunscreen aside and gave her face a couple of swipes of blusher and a dash of lipstick. Rubbing her lips together, she headed for the back door and met him in the driveway.

"Hey there," he said. "I was afraid I might be too early. I was only going tap lightly on the door in case you were still asleep."

Sam worked up a bright smile, hoping that she looked more alert than she felt.

"Coffee?"

He glanced at his watch. "Sure. A quick one. I'm on duty in ten minutes."

Before they'd quite reached the back door, he grabbed her hand and turned her around. His kiss went right to her center. She was glad she'd brushed her teeth first thing.

"Um . . . nice," he said.

Her mood shot up at least twelve points. They indulged in another kiss.

They stepped into the service porch and gave themselves over to a full-fledged full-body hug and what was about to become a real make-out session before she remembered that they both had places to be, very soon. She pushed back reluctantly and slid her hands over his muscular shoulders.

Beau straightened quickly, looking over Sam's head.

"Mom?"

Chapter 19

Sam felt her eyes go wide. Kelly was *never* awake this early. She tugged at the front of her shirt and turned toward the open kitchen door.

"Sweetie." How much had she seen? "I'd like you to meet Beau Cardwell."

He held out his hand to her pajama-clad daughter. At least Kelly had the good grace to take it.

"Deputy Cardwell is investigating the death I told you about—the artist who was buried on private land."

"Uh-huh." Kelly turned toward the coffee carafe and Sam swore she saw a little smirk on her face. She filled a mug and carried it to her room.

Sam poured a mug for Beau, topped off her own and came up with a smile. "Well. That was a little awkward."

He leaned against the counter beside the sink, drinking from his mug. "I'm sorry. I shouldn't have . . ."

"Hey, not your fault. I enjoyed it. Kelly's a big girl. She

can't pass judgment on me."

"Well, we like to think they can't. But kids always do."

"I'll talk to her later." She ran a finger along the buttons on his shirt.

"So. I stopped to see if you're available tonight? I could make dinner for us at my place?"

"Meet-the-mom time?"

"Well, I just met your daughter. Looks like the time is right." He took another sip. "Hey, let's make it a family gathering. Bring Kelly and everyone can get to know each other."

Sam ran through the list of things she had to accomplish today, including the fact that she probably wouldn't get back from Santa Fe until late afternoon. He didn't seem to mind, so they said seven o'clock and he gave her directions out to his place.

They sneaked another quick kiss on the porch and she watched him climb into the cruiser. No denying that despite her early resistance she was suddenly lusting after this guy.

She shoved that thought aside as she went back inside and peeked into Kelly's room.

"Yes, I'm interested in him. Yes, I believe he's also interested in me. Get used to it. We're going to his house for dinner tonight, where you and I will meet his mother. Get used to that, too. No attitude, okay?"

"Mom, why on earth would I have 'attitude.' He seems very nice."

Sam's suspicion meter jumped a few notches. During her growing-up years Kelly had done everything possible to chase off any man who came around. But she's an adult now, Sam reminded herself as she walked through the house, with relationships of her own and maybe she's come to realize that mom deserves the same. Even so, she knew she better brief Beau to expect anything.

No time to stress over it now. She tidied her room and looked for her watch in her jewelry box. The lumpy wood glared at her in sour yellow, until she picked up the box and moved it. Immediately, the wood warmed to her touch, the stones began to glow, and a feeling of energy surged through her. She quickly set it down and rubbed her hands together.

Bertha Martinez's words came back: "You are to possess the secret . . . the box has special powers."

She reached out and touched it again with the tip of her index finger. This was the third time she'd felt something strange from the box. When she'd first worked at Cantone's—after handling the box that morning—she'd accomplished three days' work in one. The time she'd started to massage Zoe's tired foot and the astounding reaction to her touch . . . Magic?

She drew back from it. No.

Country girls from Texas did not believe in magical powers. They believed in practical things like baking cakes and raising kids to have responsible jobs. And speaking of responsible jobs, she had leaves to rake and mouse bait to check. She pushed the wooden box to the back of the dresser and grabbed up her backpack and keys.

Outside, she put a rake and some other garden tools into the back of Zoe's Subaru and headed toward the Martinez place.

No yard had ever been raked so vigorously. She had a lot of energy to work off—thoughts of her conversation with Rupert last night, the sexual energy surrounding Beau, Kelly's continued presence in her house, and the unexplained phenomenon of the wooden box. She shook off the images and scraped leaves into several piles. By the time she'd bagged them her shakiness began to subside. Practicality took over and she realized that she'd not eaten anything all day. Food would help.

She stacked the leaf bags beside the house, to be hauled away next time she came by with her truck. A chicken sandwich on the way home gave her a shot of energy. Back home, she quickly offloaded the tools and placed a clean sheet over the floor of the hatchback's cargo area.

After a quick shower and change of clothes, she found Kelly, who gave her a hand with the wedding cake. They lifted off the top tier and made space for everything that went along with setup at the reception site. Sam draped a filmy sheet of plastic over the whole thing and was on her way.

There was something about having an almost-two hour road trip ahead. Her earlier good spirits after the morning encounter with Beau and the sense of accomplishment at finishing work at the Martinez house began to deflate as Sam thought more about what Rupert had told her last night about Cantone's estate.

She couldn't get past the idea that his nephew showed up so conveniently and that the great artist had died within such a short time. Now the nephew was living a life of riches. She just couldn't think of a way to prove anything against him. At best he might have simply been a guy who was in the right place at the right time. At worst, he might be a murderer.

There. She'd said it.

Once the word got into her head it wasn't leaving. She

chided herself for focusing so exclusively on Bart Killington, though. According to Betty McDonald there were plenty of other people who didn't much like Pierre Cantone. Money and territory were often at the root of conflicts, and she'd personally found two instances where Cantone had made someone angry. Leonard Trujillo, the neighbor who was ready to go to court over a few feet of land. What if the court had ruled against him and he decided to take out his anger on Cantone personally? Or the guy in town with that IOU for four hundred dollars—he too could have decided to take matters into his own hands. It was just that she couldn't come up with a likely way that any of the three men could have given him the pneumonia that caused his death. And who else might be out there who had a grievance with the artist?

Sam thought about it until she pulled into the wide driveway of Casa de Tranquilidad. Opening the hatch on the car and looking again at the wedding cake reminded her what life was really about. The cake, frankly, turned out beautifully. She hoped it would be one of the memorable parts of someone's wedding day. Baking and delivering beautiful things for people was the most positive part of her day, of her work in general. The minute she could get away from cleaning houses and repairing worn-down properties, she would do it. She fixed a picture of the storefront of Sweet's Sweets in her head and resolved to hold onto it.

She walked into the big resort's lobby, headed toward the ballroom, borrowed a wheeled cart from the kitchen staff and headed back to the car. A bellman helped lift the heavy lower tiers on their cake board and set it onto the cart. The smaller two tiers for the top fit nicely in place. She headed down the hall with it. The ballroom doors were closed again and she was just debating how to manage the doors and the cart when a voice piped up behind her.

"Hi again. Can I give you a hand with that?" It was the woman Sam had met on her last trip here, Charlie Parker. "Wow, beautiful cake!"

The maitre d' appeared just then and held the doors while Sam steered the cart inside.

"Oh, *there* you are," said a woman in a blue suit, the wedding planner no doubt.

"Where does this go?"

"Ah, well, the hotel staff haven't set up the cake table yet. Let's just park the cart off to the side and you can set it up after awhile."

How long a while, Sam wondered. She stood around for twenty minutes but no one seemed very organized. So, what to do? Trust that someone else could set up the cake, secure the top tiers firmly, and not touch the wrong spot and ruin something? Grrr.

Finally, she snagged the wedding planner again but the woman was interrupted three times by phone calls coming into the little headset thing she wore, like some kind of rock star diva.

Sam stood around, staring at the pictures on the walls, for another fifteen minutes. Looking at impressionist-style art made her think again of Pierre Cantone and that led her to the fact that several of his paintings were hanging in his nephew's house right now. He'd claimed there was a will but was content to bury his uncle in the backyard and leave him there. And if that young man had killed his uncle for the valuable art, it couldn't be ignored. She felt her fingers start to twitch. What if she just took a peek?

The blue-lady bustled past her again and Sam practically

stuck her foot out to stop her. "Don't let anyone touch that cake," she said. "I have an errand to do and I'll be back to set it up in about a half hour."

What was she thinking?

Before she could talk too much sense into her own head, she rushed out to the car and took off. Bart Killington's house wasn't that far away. She remembered the turns they'd made the other day and followed them. She would simply ask him to show her his uncle's will. Or, she might say that she'd been in contact with the Taos County Sheriff's office and they had questions about the will. That sounded better. But what if he called up there to verify her story? She'd be in big doo-doo with Beau and not just on a personal basis. There was surely some law against what she was about to do. Still, she drove on.

Halfway up the hill on Bart's road she spotted a car coming toward her. The green Jag. Bart was heading toward the city. She turned her head slightly and raised a hand to scratch her nose, obscuring her face from his view. He didn't even glance her way. She watched until he'd rounded a curve in the road.

Sam, it's now or never.

She accelerated up the hill and debated what to do next. Actually, she gave herself over to very little debate. At this point the only thing that would accomplish her goal was rash action. She pulled up his steep driveway, circled the portico and faced the car outward. She hadn't noticed a housekeeper or anyone else around the place the other day but her mind raced through a story that she would give if someone answered. She'd play the part of a secretary from the law firm handling the will and she needed a copy for their files, because the original had somehow become misplaced/damaged/shredded. She took a deep breath and stepped out of the car.

The front door chimes rang through a very hollow-sounding house. No response.

She placed a hand on the latch and gave it a try. It didn't just magically swing open. She eyed the lockset. How easy *that* would be. But she'd brought no tools, no picks. It wasn't going to happen.

Walking around the side of the house, Sam saw that landscapers had been hard at work, although they must have left for the day. A huge hole in the ground, criss-crossed with rebar strips, indicated that a pool was underway. Shovels stuck up out of dirt piles, boulders lay in haphazard stacks. She scanned the whole area and didn't see anyone. But she did see a low window that didn't appear securely latched.

With cupped hands she peered into the room beyond. A study, with a desk covered in papers. Right there. Just for the taking. Bart was a real fool, she decided. Without a second thought she raised the window and crawled through. No alarm sounded. A door opened into a long hall, and she took a quick peek just to be sure that there wasn't some maid standing there with a hefty dustmop in her hands.

Nothing.

A ticking clock echoed from a faraway room.

Sam gently closed the door to the study. Took a deep breath. Realized that she didn't have the luxury of taking her time. If Bart had not set the alarm he didn't plan to be gone long. She rushed to the desk and riffled through the papers. What lay out in plain sight consisted of construction invoices, notices from the utility companies, a quote for the new swimming pool. She yanked open a drawer and found about a dozen hanging file folders.

Unfortunately none of them were labeled "Will."

She flipped through them quickly. A flat tray contained incoming mail and a few other miscellaneous envelopes. It all seemed to be the average stuff that everyone gets in the mail. Drat. She'd gone through the whole stack when she came across a long, unmarked envelope at the very bottom. The flap had never been sealed; inside was a single sheet of paper. It was crisp and yet it looked worn. Odd.

It unfolded and lo-and-behold—the will.

At least it claimed to be a will. The words were there, just as Bart Killington had said, leaving the entire estate to him. There was even a shaky signature at the bottom. But the whole thing was off. No attorney had drafted this thing—they would fill at least a couple of pages with therefores and whereases before they got to the meat of any document. And the wear on the paper was superficial, like a document created recently and then buffed to look old. The date on the will purported to be twenty-five years ago, but Sam couldn't believe this paper was that old.

She stared across the room, thinking. How could her theory be proven?

Two paintings leaned against the opposite wall. More of the Cantone legacy. She stepped over and looked at the first canvas. Cantone's style, no doubt about it. She stared at them and felt renewed awe at the man's genius with paint.

She glanced back at the will, still gripped in her left hand. The signature was similar to that on the paintings, but not exact. Okay, signing a sheet of smooth paper with a pen was a different thing than signing with paint on canvas. But still . . .

So, what to do about all this? She should report the existence of the will to Beau and let him notify the proper authorities. But once they began asking questions, would this little sheet still exist?

She was looking around the room for a copier when she heard the sound.

The distinct sound of a heavy door closing.

Someone had just come through the front door. Oh god.

She sneaked a quick peek by opening the study door a half inch. She couldn't see anyone but heard a woman call out Bart's name. Carolyn Hildebrandt. Sam knew the voice. It sounded like she was standing in either the entry hall or the formal living room. Footsteps crossed the tile floor, becoming louder.

Without a thought Sam folded the envelope, stuffed it into her pocket and ran for the open window. She even remembered to close it behind her. Staying low, she crept along the back of the house. She'd passed French doors when she came in. This time she went the opposite direction, skirting the landscape boulders, aiming for the driveway and praying like crazy that she wouldn't be spotted.

She heard the woman open a back door and call out again, just as she rounded the western side of the house. Not since she'd run track in high school had Sam moved quite so fast. She fished Zoe's car keys from her pocket and jumped into the car, all in one motion. A silver Town Car was parked directly in front of one of the garage doors and she zipped around it.

There was no way Carolyn Hildebrandt didn't see the Subaru. Sam had parked right in front of the door. The art rep would have the cops on her *so* fast—Sam's heart raced at the thought.

She roared down the hill with little regard for the curves or oncoming traffic. After a quarter mile or so she began to realize how foolish that was. Wouldn't do any good to escape Hildebrandt only to die in a head-on crash. She slowed to a safe speed and gripped the wheel. By the time she reached the highway her fingers ached and her wrists felt like they had steel rods in them. She pulled to the side and braked.

Three deep breaths and her thinking cleared a little. Hildebrandt had a key to Bart's house. The greeting she'd called out had the tone of a "hi, honey, I'm home," even though Sam had not heard the exact words. What was *that* all about?

Sam shook out the tightness in her wrists and pulled out into traffic. Belatedly, she wondered whether she left things on the desk the same way she'd found them. How much of a neatnik was Bart? Would he notice minor changes? There was no point in stressing over it. She couldn't go back and fix it. Her mother always said, "Don't borrow trouble." Well, this went a little beyond that. Sam couldn't predict the fallout from her rash move, so no point in worrying over it. However, she'd created her own mess of trouble and didn't dare hope this was the last she'd hear of it.

By the time she'd returned to Casa de Tranquilidad her hands were steady again. Thank goodness. The wedding planner was in a snit because now that they had the table set up and decorated, Sam was expected to be right on the spot to set the cake in place. She did so, checked the details, and passed out business cards to a couple of hotel people who might send her some future business.

Out in the parking lot a small crowd had gathered around a Jeep and Sam immediately saw a woman down on the ground. It was Charlie, the one who'd helped with the doors earlier. She veered over to see what was wrong. Charlie was sitting up, rubbing at her head and conversing with one of the women who appeared to be a doctor. She fidgeted, wanting to stand up, so Sam extended a hand to help her. Immediately, a surge of energy flowed down Sam's arm. Charlie felt it—Sam could tell. But she didn't say anything.

The group began to disperse and Charlie caught up with her on the way back to the Subaru.

"How did you do that?" she asked. "I had a bump on the back of my head and now it's hardly there."

Sam thought of what Zoe said about how much better her aching legs felt after she'd touched them. And what Darryl said about not broadcasting this . . . whatever it is.

"I guess it's just a healing touch," she said. "I'm glad you're okay."

She got into the car and waved at Charlie as she drove off.

Now she had something else to worry about. How would she continue to answer questions like this?

Chapter 20

The drive back to Taos went by in a blur. Sam basically had to make her mind a blank, except for watching the other traffic, in order not to go completely nuts. She couldn't let herself dwell on the fact that she was now probably a felon for breaking into Bart's house and taking the envelope. And she couldn't begin to fathom what was going on with this whole 'healing touch' ability that she now seemed to possess, mainly on the days she handled the strange wooden box. All she wanted to do was bake and sell beautiful pastries to make people's lives a little happier. She didn't want to deal with a lot of mysterious stuff in her life.

She approached Taos in the middle of the town's little rush hour. Since Zoe's house was on her way home, it would be the perfect time to trade cars, if she was back from her own errands. Sam pulled into the drive that led to the back of the property, noting a couple of guest cars parked in the front. She could see Zoe, alone, through the lighted kitchen window so she tapped once and walked in, holding up her car keys.

"Hey there, you're back," Zoe said. They exchanged a few tidbits of catch-up news: she had two couples for the night but they'd walked down to the plaza for dinner at one of the nearby restaurants.

"Oh, I meant to ask you," Zoe said. "What on earth were you doing with deathcamas in your truck?"

"What?" Death something?

She held up a slack plastic grocery bag. "This was in your truck. I'll admit that I peeked."

The plant that Sam had found at the Anderson place. Cantone's place. "I was going to ask if you knew what it is. It's a peculiar shade of green."

"It's poisonous. Highly toxic to livestock and it grows wild around here."

"I found it at one of the houses I cleaned this week." Might as well admit the strange phenomena. "When I finished cleaning I saw residue of green all over the kitchen."

Zoe raised an eyebrow. "This is not something that should be in anyone's kitchen. It can kill you. Not that a person would normally eat it. According to the books, it's very unpalatable, and it would take multiple doses. But cows and sheep sometimes get into it in grazing pasture. The results aren't pretty—vomiting, frothing, convulsions."

"Whoa." A chill coursed through Sam. "I better take this to the sheriff."

"If you found it inside a house where a man died, yes, I'd do that."

Sam picked up the bag gingerly. Driving the two blocks to her house she couldn't shake the creepy feeling as Zoe's words came back to her.

Her dashboard clock told her it was 6:31 when she pulled into her driveway. There was no way she could meet Beau's mother in her current state, so she rushed inside, washed up and put on her favorite orange-gold top that Zoe claimed brought out the amber in her eyes. Kelly approved, Sam could tell. Ever since their little come-to-Jesus talk the other night, her daughter's sullenness had gone away.

They headed north of town, following Beau's directions, and passed through El Prado watching for the turn. A winding lane took them to the fenced twenty acres he'd described. Sam slowed, looking for the log pillars and carved lintel that comprised the entry. When that appeared on the right, she turned and passed a heavy log gate which he'd left open. On either side of the drive, early twilight revealed wide fields, smelling of new hay, dotted with occasional deciduous trees.

Ahead, two porch fixtures cast golden light on a log home and the windows glowed warmly. Impressive spruce trees flanked the house. She followed the driveway and parked in front of flowerbeds filled with the last of the summer's blooms. Beyond the house, a hulking wooden barn and dirt yard faded into the shadows.

Beau stepped outside, drying his hands on a towel. Two large dogs—a lab and a border collie—stared alertly from the front porch.

"Hey, you found us," he greeted. The dogs wagged with enthusiasm and he ordered them to back away.

"I hope we're not late. Things got a little crazy today."

"Hi, Kelly. Good to see you again."

She handed him the bottle of wine they'd brought. "And this is for your mother," she said, indicating one of the light cardboard pastry boxes Sam used for her business.

When had she come up with that? Sometimes the girl surprised even Sam.

"Beau? Who's out there?" The crinkly voice came out with clarity and an unexpected amount of strength.

He ushered them inside.

"Mama, it's Samantha and her daughter. Remember? I told you about them."

They walked into a homey main room with a staircase to the left. Log walls held western art and Indian blankets, there were leather couches with boldly printed pillows, and a rock fireplace which dominated one wall. Navajo rugs covered the floors. The far wall had two sets of French doors, facing toward the dark fields beyond. A dining table, now set with places for four, would overlook those views during daylight. Lamps with old leather shades gave the entire room a golden glow.

"Sam, this is my mother, Iris Cardwell. Mama, this is Samantha, and Kelly."

"Please—call me Sam," she said, shaking hands with the tiny birdlike woman who had wheeled her chair toward them.

"Honey, it's so good to meet you," Iris exclaimed. "I've been hearing Sam this and Sam that, for days and days."

"Really?" Sam sneaked a glance toward Beau.

"Mrs. Cardwell, we brought you a little something," Kelly said, handing the bakery box to the older woman.

Iris took the box with both hands and studied the purple and white label. "Well . . . my, my. Is it okay to open it now?" She lifted the flap and stared inside. "Oh! A flower garden!"

Bless her, Kelly had taken the extra cupcakes that they'd decorated for the birthday party and placed four of them into the box as a gift. It was a thoughtful gesture that obviously made Iris's day.

"I hope you like sweets," Kelly said. She took Iris's hand and gave a light squeeze.

"I love 'em. Now sit over here, honey, and let's chat."

Beau relieved her of the box and asked if Sam would like to lend a hand in the kitchen. They left the other two talking like old friends.

"How about that?" Sam said as the kitchen door closed behind them.

"Mama thinks she's about twenty, herself. It's no wonder she gets along so well with kids Kelly's age."

Sam helped him put the finishing touches on a salad and he took four good-sized steaks out to a grill on a back deck.

"While we have a few minutes, would you like the nickel tour of the house?"

They walked through the greatroom, where he pointed out some Western antiques—a saddle, an old sewing machine—that he said had come from the days when the family homesteaded land in Oklahoma. Beyond the living area a short hallway led to two bedrooms and a bathroom. Iris obviously occupied one of the rooms, where it looked like the doors had been modified to accommodate her chair.

"Let me turn the steaks and we'll finish the tour," he said.

When he returned they walked up the stairs. The master bedroom was spacious, with a king-sized bed that faced double doors leading out to a little balcony. Masculine, heavy furniture fit both Beau and his ranch lifestyle. A modern bathroom contained a huge tiled shower and wide vanity.

Male toiletry items were scattered about, not in excess.

"The whole place is just so *you*," Sam told him. "If I'd pictured the perfect environment to fit your personality, this would be it."

"Predictable, then?"

She laughed. "No, I don't see that." Their first dinner, the picnic at the gorge, certainly wasn't predictable. His bringing her, and Kelly, here to meet his mother this early in the relationship—that wasn't predictable either. She had a feeling there were a whole lot more surprises she could learn about Beau Cardwell. Including use of the occasional swear words.

"Damn! The steaks!" He dashed down the stairs and she heard the kitchen door swing back and forth on its hinges.

She followed, noting that Kelly and Iris now had their heads together over a photo album. In the kitchen, she tossed the salad and noticed that he'd put ears of fresh corn into a steamer, so she pulled them out and located a serving bowl.

"We're safe!" Beau announced, carrying in a platter of slightly charred steaks. "Luckily, Mama likes hers pretty well done. The others are mostly medium." He looked a little chagrined. "I keep forgetting where the hot spots are on that grill."

Iris kept them entertained with stories of Beau as a young boy, revealing that he'd fallen off his first horse at the age of two but luckily his father was standing by and caught him. Life was good until their ranch on the eastern plains of New Mexico was hit hard by an eight-year stretch of drought that forced the family to move to Albuquerque where Beau's father took a job he hated with the city water department. He died from a heart attack four years later.

Iris's face took on a wistful look as she spoke of her late husband. Beau seemed stoic. It was clear that family support fell to him at a pretty young age, barely out of high school.

Later, with glasses of wine on the back deck, staring into an onyx sky filled with pinpoints of diamond stars, Sam asked him about it. The dogs—he'd given their names as Ranger and Nellie—lay contentedly on their sides nearby.

"I can't be sad. I learned so many great things from my dad. Everything I know about owning and keeping this land, I learned from him. Most of what I know about how to treat a woman—even though my ex-wife has her own opinions on that. I learned what I wanted in a relationship by watching my parents. It's just that Dierdre wanted different things, like city life, society contacts, a corporate career. Nothing meshed with my style and she just couldn't citify me."

"Was it very long ago? The marriage."

"She left me more than fifteen years ago." He shrugged in his leather jacket. "It quit hurting about fifteen minutes after her car rounded the bend. Sorry, I don't mean to be flippant about it. It's just that during the whole five years of our marriage there was rarely a time that wasn't stressful. When we first met I took the stress as attraction. I learned pretty quickly that it wasn't so."

"I never married," Sam told him. She gave the quick rundown of her growing up years in Texas and the subsequent adventure in Alaska. "Call it selfish, but as long as I was raising Kelly I didn't want to share her with anyone. We had a lot of fun, just the two of us. I met men. I enjoyed some of them. I stayed as discreet as possible, never let anyone move in. But never wanted the white dress and the ring and the cake—ha! Me, who can bake a wedding cake for anyone."

"Was it a struggle?"

"Huh, you can't imagine. Well, maybe you can. I'd have to say that a sense of humor and some hard-learned street smarts have gotten me through. My dad once advised me to save as much of the money from that pipeline job as I could, and I did. I've still got a little of it, stashed away. Luckily, cause I've had to bail Kelly out of more things than I'd like to admit."

He glanced toward the closed glass door. A slight reaction. Kelly stepped out.

"Beau, Iris says she's getting tired. Is it okay if I help her get ready for bed?"

"Sure, hon, that would be nice. She can handle most of it herself, changing clothes and brushing her teeth. Just stay nearby in case she gets shaky on her feet."

Once the door closed again, Sam found herself telling him about her dream for Sweet's Sweets and how she was always just a little short on money for it. She could spend every penny of her savings and do a half-assed setup for the business, or she could save a little more and really do it right—find a prime location, get good equipment, hire some help.

"I'd go that way, if I were you," he said. "One of the things Mama didn't tell you about my dad was that he tried to keep the ranch going, longer than he should have. Spent every penny of savings, hoped each year would get better. By the time we moved to Albuquerque, it was with our last tank of gas and enough cash for four nights in the cheapest motel on east Central. We lived on peanut butter sandwiches until his first paycheck came through. And it didn't get better for a long time after that. The lesson I learned was to always keep a little buffer."

"Sounds like you and my dad would get along," she said, taking his hand.

Chapter 21

One glass of wine, the chill night air, and the long day began to catch up with Sam. When Beau caught her yawning he suggested that they go back inside. She peeked into Iris's bedroom where Kelly was sitting in a chair beside the bed, looking through a book.

"We should get going," Sam said. "Iris, good night. Thanks for having us in your home."

While Kelly looked for her purse, Sam walked out to the front porch with Beau. "It's a beautiful night," she said, enjoying the warmth of his arm around her shoulders.

"Weather's about to change. About to get some frost." He gave her a light kiss on the top of her head. "I'll talk to you tomorrow."

A discreet cough behind them and Kelly walked outside. Sam started the truck and negotiated the turn-around.

"I really liked Beau and his mother," Kelly said as they drove out through the gate. "Her stories about him as a little boy are a hoot."

"Well, she sure took to you like a ladybug to a daisy."

"Mom, where do you come up with those sayings?" She laughed as she said it.

"Grampa, I suppose. He used to say stuff like that all the time. I guess spending time with Beau and Iris brought back a lot of Texas childhood memories. You remember Grampa's farm, all those miles of cotton fields? I think of high school football games and fried chicken Sunday dinners . . .. I get around ranchers and it all comes back."

"I like him, Mom. I think he's good for you."

"Thanks, Kell."

So, what did this mean? Despite all her reservations about involvement, with her daughter's approval, Sam wondered if she was on the right track this time. She'd not had the best success at choosing men, leaning toward the ones that were good looking but too shallow to be dependable. Recognizing that, somehow, before she let them become permanent. Spending her whole life without a partner as a result.

Sam fell asleep with that train of thought and ended up having a nightmare about how her life turned out because she'd married Billy Roy Farmer and stayed in Cottonville, Texas. When she woke up to a brilliant blue New Mexico sky, with a frosty chill in the air, she felt a rush of elation. Life usually did turn out the way it was supposed to.

Yesterday's summery outfit wasn't going to cut it, she realized when she looked out to see thick frost on the neighbor's metal roof. Beau had been right about the change in the weather. She left the light blouse and pants draped over a chair and opted for socks and boots with her heavy jeans and sweatshirt.

Coffee really hit the spot. Sam stared out toward the

driveway for a few minutes, thinking again of her resolve to get Sweet's Sweets underway. The larger orders were bringing in some good money, but now she was running into the problems of working in a tiny kitchen and making cake deliveries with her pickup truck. The backseat was one of those little half-sized things, difficult to get anything in and out of, and transporting food in the open bed was out of the question. And she couldn't keep borrowing Zoe's car, especially if things turned as she hoped and she began making several deliveries a day.

On the other hand, she needed a beefy vehicle for her landscape work. At the very least, something with a trailer hitch. A mid-sized SUV or van could probably handle both needs.

Someone once told her that wishing for a thing wouldn't make it so. And yet she was a firm believer in visualizing the future. The clearer picture she could form, the more likely she was to manifest the reality. It was a technique she used in cake design all the time. Now she figured she better apply it to her business plan. The company vehicle would be a good first step. She sipped her coffee and flipped through the newspaper.

After an hour she'd come to the conclusion that her truck and all the cash in her checking account would just about make an even trade on the van she needed. She placed a couple of calls on vans that were listed for sale but both were already gone. Undeterred, she kept the image in her head while toasting two slices of bread and topping off her coffee.

Kelly emerged from her room and Sam noticed that she was shivering in her light cottons from southern California.

"I don't think I own anything warm enough for September in Taos," she said.

"You're welcome to look through my closet but I don't think anything's going to be a great fit on you." Kelly was about the size of a pencil.

She dashed into Sam's room anyway and came out with a pair of sweats that, while still large on her, were ones Sam had shoved to the end of the closet rail because they hadn't fit in years. The sweatshirt overpowered Kelly's slim frame but she seemed glad of the extra space in it.

"I'll have to do some shopping," she said.

Sam saw her bank balance take a dive.

"I've got some money, Mom. I collected my final paycheck. And there are credit cards."

Sam didn't want to get into the conversation about how she'd gotten into trouble with those cards already. The stare she sent tried to convey *get a job first*, without damaging their recent rapport

What she said was, "I'm looking at a vehicle for my business, so I'm not going to have any spare cash to help you out, Kell."

"I know, Mom. I don't expect that." She poured herself some coffee and joined Sam at the table. "Actually, I think I have a job prospect."

She saw the surprise on Sam's face.

"I talked a lot with Iris last night, and I even mentioned the idea to Beau."

Another surprise.

"You went in the bathroom right after dinner. That's when I ran the idea past him."

"What are you talking about?"

"Iris is getting pretty frail. She told me that Beau worries about her, that he runs home a few times during the day to check on her, and it's causing trouble for him at work. When anyone mentions nursing homes they both get emotional and can't talk about it." Kelly sipped at her coffee. "So, I suggested that I might become Iris's caregiver. Well, she called it a babysitter. It would just be during the day, because he's there with her at night."

"What did he think of the idea? Can he afford to pay someone?"

"Well, that's the thing. Yes. I guess he's been thinking of it for awhile but he wasn't sure about having a stranger in the house. He even interviewed a couple of women a few weeks ago but Iris didn't like either of them."

A rush of conflicting emotions ran through Sam. Kelly working for the man she was about to be romantically involved with. Would Kelly be dependable? Would they be happy with her work? Would she be happy doing that sort of thing—she'd done nothing but office work for years.

"Iris loved the idea. She wants Beau to hire me right away. He said he'd think about it, and I said I would need to run it past you."

Sam wasn't sure what to think but covered her utter surprise by carrying her empty plate to the sink and refilling her mug.

"It's quite a commitment," she said. "She'll need more and more help as she gets older."

"I know. I think I can do it. And Beau kept saying we could 'give it a try.' He probably doesn't know how his mother will react to having someone else around all the time either." She went to the cupboard and found some peanut butter crackers, which she slowly unwrapped. "At least it's something, some way for me to earn my keep until

I find out what life holds next."

"As long as you are fair with them, Kell. You can't take this job and then bail out when some high-salary corporate thing comes through." Sam held up a hand. "I'm just saying. Be sure you're ready to live up to the responsibility."

Kelly nodded. "Let's see what they say about it today. They may have changed their minds."

A few minutes of silence passed. "Kell? I'm glad you're thinking creatively about this. And I'm glad that you understand my situation and are willing to pitch in with expenses."

Kelly came over and gave her a warm hug. "Remember how it was when I was little? Just you and me. You gave up a lot for me, Mom. I don't expect you to keep doing that. I hope things work out for you and Beau."

How'd she get to be so wise? A tear threatened Sam's eye and she blinked it back.

The phone jangled on the kitchen wall and they both jumped.

"There's Beau now," Kelly said. "So, what do you think?"

"It's your choice. I know you'll make the right decision." Sam reached for the phone. "And how do you know it's Beau?"

Of course it was, and after talking to him for a minute she turned the call over to Kelly. While they discussed details, she busied herself taking inventory of her baking supplies.

"I can start tomorrow," Kelly said to Beau. Done deal.

When she hung up she said, "Now I really better find some new clothing. Looks like I'll be here for the winter." She had a huge grin on her face.

With Wal-Mart, one department store and a variety of

expensive, touristy specialty shops in town, Sam gave Kelly the options and suggested she might rather drive to Santa Fe where there was a mall and some outlet stores.

"I guess I could spend a day in the city," Kelly said. "What about you? Want to come along? I didn't even ask what you were doing when I walked in here."

Sam told her about the decision to find a new vehicle and, like the younger-thinking person she was, Kelly suggested looking online. Why hadn't she thought of that? She busied herself at the computer while Kelly dressed for her shopping trip.

"Don't spend all your money in one place," Sam kidded as she headed out the back door.

"You either!"

Back at the computer, Sam found a few possible vehicles of interest and sent emails requesting more details. While waiting for responses she figured that she better get her own truck cleaned up and ready to sell. She carried a caddy of cleaning supplies out and worked over the interior, detailing the dashboard with cotton swabs until the thing looked like it had just arrived from the showroom. Moving on to the backseat she came across the bag with the wilted stems that Zoe called deathcamas. She'd completely forgotten to mention it to Beau last night.

She set the bag in the service porch and finished cleaning the truck, inside and out.

By eleven she was more than ready for a break. If it were true that the little wooden box gave her some kind of magic energy zap, she was sure wishing she'd called upon it this morning. She put in a call for Beau, needing to tell him about the deadly plant, and then made a sandwich and flopped into a chair at the kitchen table while she waited for him to call back.

As it turned out, he stopped by instead.

"Hey, the truck sure looks spiffy," he said, giving it an admiring look.

She thanked him again for last night's steak dinner and then told him about her plan. "As much as I hate to part with it, I need the other vehicle more."

She handed him the plastic sack with the plants in it. "You told me that some kind of plant toxin showed up in Pierre Cantone's autopsy tests. I'm wondering if this might be it."

He glanced into the bag.

"They're completely crispy now, but when I first found them they seemed the same shade of green as that stuff that I found inside his house. Zoe tells me this stuff is poisonous."

He pulled out one of the stems and held it up. "Looks like deathcamas. She's right. Livestock eats this stuff and it's a horrible death. Never heard of a person eating it though. Why would they?"

"It was growing near Cantone's house. There were smears of something much like this in his kitchen. The man dies. The nephew inherits a fortune in paintings. Are you thinking what I'm thinking?"

"Anything's possible."

Sam wanted to say 'aha!' She'd not liked that nephew much anyway.

"But—" He held up an index finger. "But, to make any kind of accusation, much less a court case, we have to have some kind of proof."

"Lab tests. Can't they tell if this is the plant toxin that was in Cantone's body?"

"We can have it tested and find out. And that's a good start. But it's still a far cry from proving that the nephew administered this. Or that he didn't eat it accidentally."

"A poisonous plant like this—accidental?"

"You'd be surprised how many people experiment with plants in their yards, Sam. Some of them are tasty and harmless, like dandelion greens. They'll pick a bunch of unknown greens and make up a salad. Never put it together that they got really sick the next day."

"But day after day? Zoe said it would take quite a bit to kill a person."

"Hey, it kills horses and sheep."

Sam still couldn't see it happening accidentally to a person. "There are other people who had grudges against the man. Have you questioned Mr. Trujillo, the neighbor with the lawsuit against Anderson?"

"Haven't had time. Padilla has me on another case that just came up this morning. He's pushing hard to close the whole Anderson-Cantone file and get on to other things."

"But—" She pointed at the bag.

"I'll try. The first step would be to tie this to the victim. If I can get Padilla to agree, I'll have it tested against the toxin the lab found in Cantone. See if that tox level was high enough to be fatal. Don't count on getting a conclusive answer, though. Things like this really deteriorate with time. But we can see what happens and take it from there." He gave her a quick kiss. "I gotta get back on the job."

She walked him out to the cruiser. "Thanks for what you're doing for Kelly. The job is a big favor."

"Hey, it's a bigger favor to me. I hope she likes being with Mama. I really was getting to my wits end about a solution to the problem. I'm glad Kelly is willing to do it."

She watched him drive away, then rummaged in the garage for a For Sale sign that she'd used years ago. Filled in the phone number and a couple of details about the truck and taped it to the window. She would miss the Silverado's capacity for stuff that she had to haul away from the properties she tended, but it was time for a change.

The day had warmed up considerably, as usually happened this time of year, and Sam suddenly realized she was way too hot in her sweats. She showered and looked for something else to put on. The handiest thing was the pair of slacks and blouse she'd worn yesterday. As she pulled the pants on something crinkled in the pocket.

The envelope she'd taken from Bart Killington's house.

Chapter 22

Sam pulled the envelope from her pocket and stared at it. So much had happened in the hours since she'd been there, she'd completely forgotten to mention it to Beau. Of course, telling him about it would open another set of questions about how she'd gotten it. Maybe better to wait.

Beau's comments about both tying the plant residue to the nephew and verifying it as the cause of Cantone's death made her realize that simply finding evidence did not prove a crime. She would have to find some kind of proof that the one-page will she'd located was not the real one. Something more than her own simple intuition.

She laid the envelope on her dresser.

Back at her computer, Sam saw that she'd received a reply to one of her emails about a van for sale. It turned out that one was in Albuquerque and while she didn't relish a five-hour round trip drive to go see it, she didn't want to rule out anything either. She sent a reply thanking them for the info and saying she'd consider it.

Movement in the front yard caught her eye and she saw a man circling her truck. She stepped outside to talk to him and he readily offered about half of what it was worth. When she showed him the printout she'd gotten online with the values, he went away a little grumpy. Feeling somewhat discouraged she went back inside to find that she'd missed a call from Rupert.

When she called him back he said that he'd heard from Carolyn Hildebrandt, the art rep in Santa Fe, wondering whether Mrs. Knightly was still interested in Cantone's work. Although the painting they'd looked at was going out to New York today, she could show them some other pieces.

"I'd say, considering what we spotted in Bart Killington's house," Sam said. She didn't tell Rupert about her little breaking and entering caper the other day. You never knew what would end up in one of his books.

"So, would you like to become Mrs. Knightly again and run to Santa Fe for the day?" he asked.

She considered it for about half a second. The drive down to the capital was getting old. Plus, what would they really learn? She already knew that Hildebrandt and Bart were close, and she was pretty certain that Bart's stash of Cantone paintings were the real thing, art that he'd taken from the artist's Taos residence. She begged off, using her caretaker job as an excuse.

Rupert grumbled a little and she suspected that he'd secretly wanted to take the day off from his writing. But like most professionals, he was pretty good about disciplining himself to devote a certain number of hours a day to his craft, and like it or not he sometimes needed for his friends to not enable his lazy streak. He said as much before ending the call.

Well, thought Sam, I guess I could say the same for myself. Can't very well nag Rupert about not working if I don't do the same. As she placed her gold hoop earrings into the lumpy wooden box she had a thought. If the box seemed to give her an energy boost, why not use that to her advantage?

She picked it up and held it in her arms, close to her body. Again, warmth surged from the wood and the yellowish surface began to radiate golden light. The stones glowed more brightly than she'd ever seen them. She quickly set the box back on her dresser, her heart pumping. The power of the thing unnerved her.

She stared at it for a couple of minutes.

You might be playing with fire, Sam.

Shaking her hands to dispel the tingly feeling in them, she began to back out of the bedroom. Then something green caught her eye.

The envelope containing the purported will.

The entire surface of the envelope was covered in smears of the greenish, powdery substance. The same thing Sam had seen in Cantone's kitchen, the stuff Rupert swore he couldn't see.

She picked it up and gingerly opened the flap. Inside, the single sheet of paper also had green marks on it.

Bart Killington was definitely connected to the green dust now.

She dropped the envelope on the dresser and grabbed up the telephone.

"Beau, there's something weird going on here."

While he went through a whole bunch of "are you okay?" kind of stuff, she gathered her thoughts. Working at sounding rational, she told him about taking the envelope from Killington's house and how she'd found powdery green marks on it, just like those at the house that she suspected to be deathcamas.

"It ties the nephew to the poisonous plant—don't you see?" she insisted.

Beau took a long breath. "It ties a green substance to both the envelope and the kitchen of the house, Sam. First, we'd need a lab analysis to verify that the green is from deathcamas. And, we still don't know that the uncle didn't pick those plants himself and carry them into the house. He might have sat at that kitchen table to write out the will."

Sam bristled. How could she explain the feeling she got when she touched that envelope?

"Sam, it doesn't prove any kind of foul play by the nephew. Don't you see that I wouldn't have anything at all that I could take to a prosecutor? I'm in my office today," he said. "Bring me the envelope with the will and I'll see what kind of tests we can run on it. Maybe we can get someone to analyze the signature, if nothing else."

Fifteen minutes later, she'd hopped in her truck and was on her way downtown to the Sheriff's Department. All the way there, she debated what to say. In the end she decided the whole truth was the only way.

"Can we talk privately?" she asked as soon as he appeared.

"Sure." He ushered her out into a small courtyard. They sat on concrete benches in the shade.

She laid out the whole story, starting with the day that Bertha Martinez had given her the wooden box. "The rumors you heard about her being a witch. I'm beginning to think maybe they were true," she said. "How else can I explain the weird stuff that's been happening to me ever since I got that box?" He leaned back, letting her finish the story.

She told him that she'd not noticed the green marks in the Cantone house that first day—probably because she'd hardly touched the box—but on other occasions when she'd actually rubbed her hands over the box she'd been almost hyper-aware, seeing the green residue.

"That's what happened this morning, Beau. The day I found this envelope I hadn't handled the box. Today, after I touched it, the marks became as clear as anything."

"And you still see them now?" he asked, holding it up.

"Yes! They're almost brilliant green."

To his credit, he didn't laugh and he didn't freak out and leave her sitting there. He shook his head slowly and she felt disheartened. He noticed her expression. "Sam, it's not that I don't believe you. I know you to be honest and sincere. It's just that this isn't something we can use to build a case. The prosecutor would laugh me out of his office, *if* Sheriff Padilla even let me go that far. And even the worst defense attorney would tear the case to shreds."

He was right of course. She knew that.

"But you could build a case based on lab proof that the poisonous plant toxin was in the house and on the will. And I'll bet it's the same plant toxin the lab showed in Cantone's body. Please, Beau, please come out there with me. I'll show you where it is and you gather the evidence."

She felt his hesitation. "What?"

"I'm supposed to be working on this other case now." He lowered his voice. "Padilla is already hassling me about this. It's an election year. He's a political animal and he knows his chances of being re-elected hinge on people's perception that crime is under control. If a death can be ruled an accident and quietly filed away, that's how he wants it. If a case gets sent to the prosecutor, it better be a damn strong one—something that makes Padilla look good."

"But surely he doesn't want people getting away with murder! If we could get the evidence . . ."

He gave a thin smile. "It would be a start. But as I've told you before, we would have to prove that the nephew administered the poison and we'd have to prove intent to kill his uncle."

"But at least it's something," she said. "I can't stand the idea of that poor old man dying such a horrible death and this greedy nephew burying him in a hidden grave and walking away with a fortune."

"I agree about that," he said. "The whole thing really stinks."

He stood up and they walked back to the office. "Okay. An hour, tops. I'll say it's my lunch break. Let me get a lab technician to come with us. The other thing we have to do here is make sure that there are more than just the two of us gathering this evidence. You're already going to have some explaining to do about how you got that envelope from Killington's house. And if all the evidence comes from my girlfriend, that's another thing a defense attorney will jump on like a dog on a bone."

Girlfriend?

He'd picked up the phone and punched a two-digit intercom extension. "Lisa, can you take your lunch break now? I need you to bring your lab kit and come with me. Five minutes, my office."

While they waited for Lisa, Beau stared at the envelope Sam had handed him.

"You still see green all over this?" he asked.

"You don't? Nothing at all?"

"It looks like a white envelope and the page inside looked like plain old paper," he said. "Sam, I'm so sorry I can't verify it for you."

She gave a dispirited shrug. What else could she say? She didn't want this ability to see and feel things that no one else could experience, and she knew they couldn't be expected to believe her just because she said so. She suddenly realized that her life would never be the same, as long as she possessed that damned wooden box.

Chapter 23

Beau followed her red truck out the county road and up to the Cantone property. Sam waited as he and Lisa got out of his cruiser, then she unlocked the front door and led the way into the house. The place smelled of loneliness. She tried to imagine how it must have been when Cantone first moved in. Had he immediately set up his work area and begun some new paintings? Had the house held a vibrancy because of the old man's creative energy? If so, it was gone now.

"Take your time and tell me each place we should test," Beau said.

Sam wondered how much of her story he'd explained to Lisa on the way out here. The tall girl with cropped dark hair and pale skin didn't comment on anything. She set the lab kit down on the living room floor and opened the lid, busying herself by pulling out some bottles and swabs. A stack of small evidence envelopes went in one pocket of the apron she'd put on.

Sam walked slowly through the living room, finding one semi-circular green mark on an end table.

"Here," she said. "It's about the size and shape that a wet drinking glass might make." The green was much more vivid than what she'd seen on the envelope with the will in it.

Lisa took a clean swab and ran it over the area Sam indicated, then placed the swab into one of the little envelopes.

They moved on into the dining room, but Sam didn't spot any marks there. The kitchen was just as she'd left it the last time—green swipe marks on the table and countertop. Faint traces showed near the drain, and Sam remembered washing dishes there, running quite a lot of water down the drain as she cleaned the place. She was amazed that any residue was left at all, she told Beau.

On to the bedrooms. In Cantone's room she didn't find any trace of the green. A glance toward the open closet reminded her that she still needed to get some paint and cover the drywall patch where they'd cut the small mural out. In the second bedroom her pulse quickened.

"Beau, it's all over the place in here."

"Do any of them look like fingerprints?" Lisa asked. "Point those out to me."

Bless the girl, Sam thought. She didn't question.

Sam spotted green prints at the light switch and on the back edge of the door. Lisa quickly pressed fingerprint tape over them and lifted them off.

"Here's something that could be a handprint," Sam said. "Well, part of one."

She showed them the area and Lisa lifted that as well.

"Some of the smudges on the furniture are blurry. Probably my fault. When I cleaned the house I dusted everything." She looked up at Beau. "Sorry. I didn't see the marks that first day."

"It's okay. You're finding some good stuff now. We'll be able to compare the prints in various parts of the house with what's on the will. At least connect those. Unfortunately, we weren't able to get very good prints from the body because of decomposition. But we can certainly get them from the nephew."

He asked Sam to go through the entire house once again, paying attention to anyplace she hadn't noticed earlier. On the back of the kitchen door she saw the clearest prints yet, a full palm print and fingers that wrapped around the edge of the surface. As if someone had pulled the door closed as he left.

While Lisa packed up her lab kit, Sam asked Beau if he thought the information was valuable to solving the case.

"First off, the lab will test to verify this is the fatal poison. That way, if the prints are Bart Killington's we can tie him to the poisonous plant. That's something. I'm going to have to find a plant expert who can give us an idea whether there is enough of the substance here to be fatal. If not, all Bart has to do is claim that yes, he picked some of the plants and then came inside and touched a variety of places in the house."

"But the green stuff is also on the will," Sam pointed out.

"That's certainly more damning," Beau admitted. "But we already know that Bart handled the page and the envelope. It was in his house."

"But the poison wasn't in his house . . ." She paused. "Actually I don't know that. I couldn't *see* the green in his house. I only spotted it on the will today, after I handled the box again."

Beau gave her a stern look. "Do not go back there on your own, Sam. Not unless you want to admit to breaking and entering, which is going to get you into a whole bunch of trouble."

She fumed. Wasn't she already in trouble on that score?

Beau and Lisa were headed for the door.

"Is it okay if I clean the place thoroughly now?" Sam asked, as he lingered to say goodbye. "It doesn't seem smart to leave a poisonous residue around the house now that there could be potential buyers coming to look at it."

"We've got everything we can use," he said. "Go ahead."

She surreptitiously squeezed his hand and watched with mixed emotions as he walked out to the cruiser. She knew he was just doing his job when he cautioned her about going back to Bart's place in Santa Fe, but still . . . she felt strongly that Cantone's nephew was about to get away with murder.

She spent two hours vigorously scrubbing away the traces of green, hoping the scientific tests would back up her intuition.

The afternoon was still young, with a brilliant September sky and the leaves on the cottonwoods showing a hint of the golden autumn yet to come. She grabbed a chicken sandwich at the first café she came to, then headed up the ski valley road to check on her property up there—the only one of her current three that hadn't thrown a huge dose of drama at her. A quick check verified that all was well there.

She drove home as the shadows were lengthening across

the valley and found Kelly's car in the driveway, back from her clothing foray in the city.

"Hey, Mom." Kelly greeted as Sam walked into the kitchen. Her blue-green eyes sparkled. "Wait till you see—I got some great bargains at the mall."

"Good." Sam automatically glanced at the light on the answering machine, hoping for another bakery order to add to the week's income. Nothing.

"Everything okay?" Kelly was pouring pretzels from a bag into a small bowl. She held it up to Sam, who waved away the snacks.

"Yeah, fine." She wasn't ready to go into the whole story of her involvement with the investigation.

Kelly carried the pretzels to the kitchen table, where several large plastic bags appeared to be stuffed with clothing. "Look at these." She proceeded to pull out slacks and sweaters, a warmup suit and a puffy winter coat, holding each item up to herself to show how it would look. "I found most of these on sale racks. Amazing, at this time of year."

Sam put on a happy face and worked to let go of the nagging concerns about Cantone and his crooked nephew. She congratulated her daughter on her clothing buys.

"Shall we have the rest of that pasta you made the other night?" she asked, as Kelly started to carry her purchases to her room.

She studied her hands to be sure she'd washed off every trace of the green dust. All clear. Preoccupied with thoughts of that, she pulled pasta and sauce from the fridge and poured two glasses of wine. Kelly came back into the kitchen to slice and butter bread and spread it with garlic. While the bread toasted, they raised their glasses.

"I'm really excited about my new job," Kelly said as she

set the table. "Iris seems like such a sweet lady."

"I hope it works out well—all the way around," Sam told her. As much as she wanted to add some motherly advice about working hard and doing her best for Beau and his mother, she held her tongue. Realizing that Kelly had been out on her own for a long time was a hard thing to accept. But if Kelly messed up, her own chances with Beau might be finished.

The phone interrupted her thoughts, just as they were finishing their dinner. An order for a specialty cake. The customer's daughter was celebrating her quinceañera and the family wanted to do it up big. Sam suggested a tiered cake, which always made a girl feel like a bride, and she could color-coordinate figures of the girl's attendants to the dresses they would wear in the actual ceremony. The longer they talked, the more elaborate the cake became and the woman didn't flinch when Sam quoted her the price. It was only after she'd hung up that Sam began to wonder if she could pull it off.

Okay, she told herself, it's not very different than a wedding cake and you've done plenty of those. She could order the figurines online tonight and they would be shipped tomorrow, arriving in a couple of days. She had a supply of risers and separators, to set off the elegant tiers. The cake wasn't needed for a week yet, so she had plenty of time to get her supplies lined up and pre-make most of the flowers and other decorative elements that needed time to set up. She grabbed a pencil and sheet of paper and began to sketch out the design as the idea took hold. A success here could very well secure her a lot of business among the Hispanic families in town, and it would be worth her while to give this one a lot of attention.

She drifted into the living room and sat at her computer desk in the corner, getting her supply order done in no time. A quick check of her email and she saw two more responses to her queries about vans for sale. One was in Eagle Nest, a small village about forty minutes away, on the other side of the mountains. A quick phone call, the right answers to her questions, and she told the seller that she would drive over in the morning to take a look.

As if the cosmos had heard her plea for more bakery business, the phone rang again, Ivan at the bookstore reminding her of their annual open house tomorrow evening. He wanted to know if she could deliver their cake by mid-afternoon. Sam's knees almost buckled. He'd spoken to her about the event almost a month ago and she'd completely forgotten. She put a smile in her voice and reassured him.

"Kelly! Help!" she yelled, the second the phone disconnected. "I've got to turn out a special cake—tonight!"

Sam flipped through her recipe box for her special red-velvet. Since everything she baked at Taos's 7,000 foot elevation required special altitude adjustments, she didn't dare use a recipe from any old cookbook. "Can you whip this up and get it into the oven now?" she said, handing the card over to Kelly.

Bless her heart, Kelly didn't skip a beat. She turned the oven dial to preheat and began pulling ingredients from the shelves. Sam muttered as she reached into her storage cabinets on the service porch. There were book-shaped pans somewhere in here and that would be the perfect thing for the store's needs. After a heart-pounding moment in which she began to wonder if she'd given the pans away, she found them. Two pans, representing the halves of an open book. The overall size would be nearly twenty-five inches wide and three inches thick.

"Wash these out before you use them," she told Kelly. "And as soon as you get the cake into the oven, we need the mixer for a batch of buttercream."

Sam pulled another large mixing bowl from the shelf and the moment Kelly had finished beating the cake batter, Sam washed the beaters and started on the icing. As she whipped the creamy mixture to piping consistency she visualized the finished confection.

The cake would be an open book on a large board. Ivory frosting for the pages, a brown border to look like a leather cover, and she could dust on a whisper of edible gold powder to make the page edges appear gilt. Ivan's favorite book of all times was Dickens' *Tale of Two Cities* and she would borrow the opening line and pipe it on one of the cake's open pages . . . "It was the best of times . . ." Roses in the store colors of burgundy and gold, with deep green leaves, would add drama and elegance.

She spooned out lumps of frosting for each of the colors. A tiny hint of brown to create the ivory, a small amount to be tinted green for the leaves, another little bit made black for the writing, and a good-sized glob that would become the burgundy roses. She worked them first, piping them onto small squares of waxed paper and setting them onto a cookie sheet to harden in the refrigerator. A few half-sized ones became rosebuds.

When the oven timer dinged to signal that the cake was done, the two women stared at each other in relief.

"That was a miracle," Sam said. She set the timer again

to remind her when to remove the cakes from the pans. At that point she set them on cooling racks on the service porch counter, to cool a little more quickly.

Kelly glanced up at the kitchen clock. Ten-fifteen. "Oh, boy. I better get to bed. I'm supposed to report for my new job at seventy-thirty in the morning."

"Thanks for your help, Kell. I couldn't have done all this without you."

"Sure, Mom." She sent a little kiss across the room.

Sam debated whether to try to finish the cake before retiring, herself, but decided that she was too tired. The day was catching up to her quickly.

In her room, she looked at the wooden box on her dresser. Like her own energy, the colors had faded once more.

Chapter 24

Twelve hours, Sam calculated. That was about how long the power of the box seemed to stay with her. She fell into bed, completely exhausted.

The alarm woke her Saturday morning. She'd remembered to set it, thank goodness, or she'd never get everything done today. She rushed to the kitchen and retrieved the cooled cake from the service porch. By the time Kelly appeared at seven, the ivory frosting was in place and Sam had scratched lines along the sides of it to represent the pages of the book.

She wished Kelly a good day on the new job and insisted she at least take along a granola bar or something to give her the energy to start the day.

Sam caught herself yawning as she dusted the edges of the pages with edible gold powder. Maybe it would help if she went in and held the magic box for awhile. She stopped herself. What if the thing were somehow addictive? What if she got so used to the energy it gave off that she couldn't get through the day without it? The thought scared her. She brewed some coffee instead and downed a cup before proceeding with the cake.

By eight-thirty, she'd finished the wording and flowers and was putting the large sheet into the spare refrigerator to cool thoroughly and set up nicely before delivering it.

Still feeling like she was moving in slow motion, she scrambled a couple of eggs for herself and made a sandwich with them on whole wheat toast. She would not depend on the wooden box for energy.

Beau called just as she was finishing her sandwich.

"Hey there." He had a sultry tone in his voice and she guessed that he wasn't calling from home or office. They exchanged a few suggestive ideas that might have actually gone somewhere (she was home alone for a change), but he said he was up to his eyebrows in paperwork today and she was, almost literally, up to hers in frosting.

"Just wanted to let you know that we got the tox reports back on the tissue that the M.I. took from Cantone's body. Your plant—the deathcamas—matches."

"Oh gosh." Sam got a sinking feeling. No matter how much her gut told her that Cantone had been murdered, she'd really hoped that he was merely an old man who got sick and didn't recover. The idea that his own nephew killed him and buried him was repugnant.

"We still don't have that proof," Beau reminded her when she voiced her thoughts. "But I'm going to try to work with Santa Fe County to get Bart Killington brought up here for questioning. I'll let you know how it goes."

She cleaned the decorating tools and put everything away, thinking about Beau and wondering what questions he would ask Bart. The guy was so smooth, she couldn't imagine him just buckling down to confess. But you never knew.

A quick call to Ivan, who said he was ready to take delivery on the cake, and she was out the door. His helpers at the bookstore were thrilled when she carried the cake in and set it on a table they'd prepared for it.

"Sam, you are the best!" Ivan said, bowing as he handed her a check. "Cake is better than I ever expect. The customers are to love it!"

Before leaving, she confirmed with him that the Chocoholics would be meeting again on Tuesday. He suggested another book-shaped cake for them, smaller, and done all in chocolate. She assured him she could do it.

On the front sidewalk there was a flurry of activity as Sam walked out. Two men were in a heated argument next to the bookstore, in front of a gourmet shop where Sam occasionally bought flavorings. She'd nearly passed them when a phrase caught her attention.

"I'll have the Sheriff's people out here with an eviction notice," the shorter of the two men yelled.

"Well, go ahead," said the other, turning on his heel. He nearly bumped into Sam, muttering under his breath, "Good luck in finding me."

She sent a tentative smile his way but he'd already walked back into the shop and slammed the door.

Sheriff's office, huh. Poor Beau, he must get every crummy job out there. She thought of him trying to solve murder cases while stepping in to deliver eviction notices and who knew what else.

She got to her truck and decided to give Rupert a call. "How would you like to skip out on writing for awhile and take a mountain drive with me?" she asked.

He agreed so speedily that she could only guess that Victoria DeVane's characters were giving him fits.

She picked him up ten minutes later and they drove east on Kit Carson Road. The winding drive put her in a bucolic mood and she gave herself over to enjoying the brilliant yellow black-eyed Susans and purple asters that lined the pavement. Elm trees cast dappled shadows over the occasional adobe cottages and log cabins that appeared along the winding Rio Fernando.

Rupert was in a chatty mood and he kept Sam entertained with stories about the celebrities who'd attended an art academy fund raiser the night before. She laughed at the right places, embarrassed to admit that she didn't recognize half the names and wouldn't have known any of the faces. She probably hadn't looked at an issue of *People* in five years, and her days of avidly following who was who had waned soon after the Beatles broke up. But Rupert was in his element in that environment.

They crested Palo Flechado Pass at more than 9200 feet and started down the opposite side of the mountain, the ski runs of Angel Fire visible in the distance. Ten miles through a wide green valley took them past Eagle Nest Lake, which sparkled in the midday light, and into the little town of Eagle Nest. Sam always marveled at how different this terrain was than her side of the mountain, only a few miles away. They cruised the main street with its quaint western-styled shops and restaurants, and then found the turnoff the man had described. In a plain little residential neighborhood sat a white van parked beside a house with wood siding, which was painted tan and green.

"This looks like the place," she said, pulling in behind

the van. Her eyes sparkled. The vehicle looked like exactly what she wanted.

"Honey, you better tone down the enthusiasm. The guy's going to double the price."

"Ah, but he already quoted it in his ad," she pointed out.

Rupert shrugged and got out of the truck.

An older man came out of the house, hitching up his jeans and making tucking motions at a red plaid shirt that was already tightly tucked in.

"Howdy. Bill Hutchins." His voice immediately reminded Sam of her father. She greeted him in the same tone. They went back and forth with a little where-are-you-from chat and learned that they'd grown up less than fifty miles apart. He'd bought the small van because his wife loved antiquing and wanted to open a shop. They'd planned to make buying trips all over the area but then she'd broken her hip last winter and it soon became clear that the business would never get off the ground. He'd decided to sell the van since it was a painful reminder to his wife that her dream wasn't going to happen.

"I want to take her on a cruise," he said. "Them ships got ever'thing now. She'll like that, gettin treated like a queen."

Sam circled the van while he talked. It truly was perfect for her needs. There were back seats but they folded down to create a large cargo area. A remote opener gave hands-free access to the back, a huge help when she was loaded down with a big cake. It even had a trailer hitch already mounted, which would allow her to hook up her utility trailer and continue with her caretaking job. And it still smelled new.

"I like it a lot. I just have to work out the money part,"

she told Hutchins, waving toward the big red Silverado. "I brought cash for a deposit but then I have to sell my truck."

He gave a little frown. "It's just that I got her listed online, you know?"

Sam caught a glimpse of Rupert, signaling her from the front of the van. She excused herself and walked over to him.

"Sam, how much are you short?"

"I need ten thousand, and it really has to come from selling the truck."

"Why? You might need the truck sometimes too. Let me give you the money. You can use two vehicles."

"Absolutely not! You can't do that."

"Honey, Victoria makes more money than I can spend. I've got money with me . . ."

She looked again at the van and at Bill Hutchins. "I can't really ask him to hold it for me, can I?"

"No. And it's perfect for you." Rupert's enthusiasm tugged like a tidal wave. "I'm seeing your Sweet's Sweet logo, done in that technique that covers the whole vehicle."

"Oh, no. Something small and tasteful," she insisted. Here she was, planning a paint scheme already?

Rupert nudged her. "Tell him you want it."

Sam wavered. Technically, she could take the money from her savings but she would lose interest on it and she'd promised herself that money would go toward equipping her bakery kitchen. Her truck was in good shape and it should sell quickly. "Only if we call it a loan. I'll pay you the minute I sell the truck."

"Fine." He looked like he really didn't care how long it took.

They consummated the deal and Hutchins signed over the title. Sam nearly choked when Rupert pulled out a wad of hundreds but she didn't say anything in front of the other man. Hutchins pocketed the cash, shook hands and went back in his house.

"I saw a cute burger place on the main drag," Sam told Rupert as they were about to get into the two vehicles. "Let me buy you lunch."

Rupert was never one to pass up a hearty meal, she'd noticed, and he grinned at the suggestion. He climbed into the Silverado and she took the wheel of her new van. They parked in front of the '50s-themed burger place a few minutes later.

"So, Rupe, don't tell me that you always carry that kind of cash on you."

He shrugged. "Actually, never. I just went prepared to the art fundraiser last night and then I didn't buy anything."

"Thank you." She stood on tiptoe and gave him a long hug. "You're a wonderful friend."

Sam found herself in a mellow mood driving back over the mountain, after devouring thick, juicy burgers and freshly cut fries. They parked both vehicles at her house and she gave Rupert a lift home in her new van, hugging him again before he got out.

Beau had left a message on her machine at home and she called him back. He let her go on for a minute or so about the great vehicle find before she remembered to ask him what he'd called about.

"I spent the morning in Santa Fe, questioning Bart Killington."

"Really? And?" She held her breath in hopes that the case had been neatly wrapped up.

"And not much," he said. "He swears he knows nothing about any poisonous plant, that he never harmed his uncle."

"Bull! I just don't believe it."

"I don't know, Sam. I've questioned a lot of people over the years. This guy's whole demeanor just seemed truthful."

"You're kidding! He admits he was living in the house with Cantone. Residue of the plant is all over his bedroom. The kitchen fairly reeked of the stuff. That had to be the place where he ground up the plant and added it to the old man's food or drink or whatever."

"Sam, he was even willing to give fingerprints so we could check for a match."

"Really?" She felt a flicker of uncertainty. "And?"

"The prints of plant residue that we lifted don't match Bart Killington."

Chapter 25

Sam felt an almost physical shock. "Did you say they *don't* match?"

"Don't. Do not. The prints aren't Bart's."

What could that mean? Maybe the prints belonged to the artist himself and maybe he really had picked the plants and eaten them. What other explanation could there be?

". . . and should have an answer in the next day or two," Beau was saying.

"Sorry. I didn't catch all of that."

"Prints from Cantone's body. We've got an expert coming in, a guy who knows more about getting partial prints from other places—wrists, palms of hands, and such." His voice softened. "Sam, you can't let this get to you so much. It's probably the hardest thing in law enforcement, not to force the evidence to fit the outcome we want. But we can't do that. You may not like the answers but whatever they are, they'll be the truth."

She forced herself to breathe slowly and counted three beats before she responded.

"I know, Beau. I know."

"We can re-examine the motives of those other suspects, the neighbors Cantone didn't get along with. They'd all have access to the plants, and maybe one of them was a whole lot angrier than we realized. But frankly, Sam, those possibilities seem thin. I'm thinking the old guy probably accidentally ingested the stuff."

She hung up feeling a huge letdown, puzzling over the new twist. Just when she was about to call Beau back to ask more questions, she noticed that a car had pulled up out front and a man was walking toward her truck. She gave him a minute to circle it and when he stayed she went out to greet him.

"I've been wanting a truck like this ever since we moved here," he said. "We're up on a dirt road in the hills and that sedan just doesn't make the climb whenever it's wet out."

"She's good in snow, too," Sam said, wondering whether she'd miss her old 4x4 when it was gone.

She opened the door for him and he sat inside, clearly enjoying himself. Then he looked under the hood and prodded the tires to see how much tread they had left. Twenty minutes later they'd worked it out that he would give her a check for the full amount now and leave the truck with her. Monday they'd meet at the bank, cash the check, she'd sign over the title.

She took the For Sale sign off the truck then called Rupert to let him know that she could repay his loan by Monday afternoon.

"I don't know what to think now about Pierre Cantone's death," she said, after telling him what Beau had said about the non-matching fingerprints. "Maybe I completely misjudged Bart."

"Well, I still think he's one cold fish," Rupert said. "I mean, anyone who could stick a relative into a grave in the backyard and then go off and start spending his fortune. The man's dirt. At least he could have sprung for a decent funeral."

"Maybe you should be saying that to him."

"Maybe I will."

A lightbulb came on. What if . . . "I'm thinking we should pay Bart Killington a little social visit. If he knew that people in the art world are upset about Cantone's unseemly gravesite, maybe he actually would feel some remorse. Maybe he'd feel honor bound to do a nice memorial." And maybe she could find some other evidence to nail the sick little creep, if she could just get inside his house again.

"Mrs. Knightley . . . you have standing in the art world. A leisurely Sunday drive tomorrow, my dear?"

"Bring me something to wear again."

This time Sam's outfit was a chic pantsuit in autumn gold, with strappy sandals and again the Patek Philippe. As she bent to buckle the sandals she eyed Rupert's feet. What size . . .? nah—she refused to think about it.

Before he arrived she'd prepared by holding the wooden box in her arms, and again she felt an almost tingly sensation in her hands when she set it down. Her hair behaved perfectly when she brushed it and, again, she swore her skin looked fresher and younger. She pushed the box to the back of her dresser. She could not let herself get in the habit of relying on its power.

Rupert had called ahead to Carolyn Hildebrandt and set an appointment, saying that Mrs. Knightly wanted to view more of Cantone's work. The plan was to find nothing of interest at the gallery and insist on being shown more. Hildebrandt would be their ticket into Bart's home. And Sam would keep her eyes open for anything with that odd shade of green powder on it.

The plan worked like a charm, right up to the moment Bart Killington opened his door to them.

"We've met, haven't we?" he said, staring hard at Rupert.

Sam gulped. They hadn't planned on his being there.

"Why, my goodness, I think we have. The day my Land Rover broke down on this road. You were so kind as to let me use your phone."

Bart was giving Sam the stare now but she could tell he seemed puzzled. "Do you have an older sister?"

"Yes!" Rupert jumped in. "Yes, Mrs. Knightly's sister. I was giving her a ride to the airport that day. You have an excellent memory, Mr. Killington." He sounded almost flirtatious and Sam wanted to nudge him in the ribs.

Instead, she turned to Carolyn Hildebrandt. "The paintings?"

"Bart?" Hildebrandt clearly wanted to get to the bottom line as quickly as possible. She'd had to lock up her gallery for this.

"Oh yes. Well. Most of them aren't hanging yet. As I think I mentioned before, I've just moved in."

"Show Mrs. Knightly the two in the dining room," Rupert said, sticking with the cover story.

Bart led the way and Sam reverted to script with lots of 'interesting' and 'I must consider this one' thrown in. She hardly noticed the paintings themselves. Both frames had faint smudges of green on the edges.

"There are more in my safe. If you'll take seats in the living room, I think Ms. Hildebrandt and I can carry them in for you." They bustled away.

Once the other two were out of sight, Sam began to wander the room, looking for any signs of the green residue. There didn't seem to be any. Not surprising. Bart had moved to this house a couple of months after his uncle's death. Only items that had previously been in Cantone's home were likely to yield any clues. She scurried back to the couch when she heard voices in the hall.

Hildebrandt entered, carrying a fairly large landscape, gripping the heavy wood frame by its edges. Behind her, Bart held two smaller pieces by the wires on the backs. They propped the three paintings against a wall, apologizing again that they weren't properly hung for viewing. Sam gave Rupert a subtle shake of her head.

"It's no problem," Rupert assured them. "I don't think we see anything of interest in this group. Would you like for us to come with you to take a quick peek at the others?"

Bart didn't seem to like the idea of showing them where his safe was, but he wasn't thrilled at having to haul all the paintings through the house either. Hildebrandt shot him a look and he capitulated.

"Come this way," he said.

They followed him down a long hall and into his study. One of the bookcases along the wall had been pushed aside to reveal a walk-in safe behind it. Sam eyed the mechanism appreciatively. She'd had no idea this existed on her previous visit.

The paintings which had been stacked against the wall

that day were now inside the safe. She stood in the doorway while Bart stepped inside and shifted the canvases to reveal each new one. Of the dozen paintings, four of them had distinct green marks on them—six, including the two hanging in the dining room.

"There's something special about those," Sam said, pointing to the four with the marks.

Hildebrandt responded with all the usual art-talk, comments on the artist's techniques, his style. But no one seemed to notice the smudges. Certainly, neither Bart nor Carolyn made a move to wipe away what would have appeared to be dust, if they could see it. Sam glanced at Rupert. He was clearly enthralled at seeing so many works by his favorite artist, all in one place. But he evidently didn't see any unusual markings either.

"Rupert," Sam said, interrupting his reverie, "wasn't there something you specifically wanted to speak with Mr. Killington about?" She sent a pointed stare his direction.

Comprehension dawned. Rupert drew himself up straight. "Yes, there was." He turned on Carolyn Hildebrandt. "I'm shocked that you haven't pressed this matter, as someone with standing in the art world."

Puzzlement from both Bart and Carolyn.

"A number of us are very upset that Pierre Cantone received such a primitive burial, and even more distressed that there was no memorial service for him. At the very least all of Santa Fe and Taos should have been told of his death. We are mourning deeply, nay, profoundly at the loss to the art world. And nothing . . . nothing! . . . to memorialize such a great man."

Okay, Rupe, Sam thought. Chill just a little.

But the great man was not to be shushed.

"I'm prepared to purchase—for my own collection—and I am not opposed to compensating you at full market value. But there must be a suitable tribute to the immortal Cantone."

He turned to Sam, throwing the ball squarely in her court.

"Absolutely," she said, as adamantly as she could muster. "Without a proper burial and suitable memorial . . ."

Carolyn Hildebrandt recovered first. "But of course."

Bart seemed to be hanging on to his first story. "My uncle's wishes, though . . . He loved his land, the open space."

Sam stared him down. In full Mrs. Knightly mode her voice dripped ice. "Surely, Mr. Killington. Surely there is an appropriate open space that might be utilized. In fact," she paused as an idea hit her. "In fact, it seems that part of the proceeds from the sale of Cantone's work should be used to purchase the property on which he lived. To recreate his studio, to hang many of his works, and to lay out a proper grave site for him."

The silence practically reverberated in the small room.

Rupert stared at her for a good four seconds before his mouth would work again. "Sa— Say, what an excellent idea! I mean, surely the sale of just one or two paintings would procure the site, cover the necessary upgrades for renovation and security measures . . .. And of course a trust should be set up for the ongoing care and maintenance of the place." He faced the open room and waved one hand in an arc. "I see it now, The Pierre Cantone Foundation for the Furtherance of Art Studies."

Bart's face had gone white. Carolyn's wheels were clearly

turning, figuring out how she could score commissions on the whole plan.

Sam took in the whole tableau, enjoying the drama.

After a good thirty seconds passed without a word, Sam shook herself out of it. She'd come here to find evidence of a murder and ended up starting an art foundation?

Chapter 26

Carolyn Hildebrandt finally spoke, her voice bright with the prospect of several sales. "Well, I'd say this calls for some champagne!"

Bart's arms flapped uselessly at his sides, like he couldn't comprehend what had just happened.

Sam felt a glow of satisfaction. With a well-known gallery owner behind the idea, he couldn't very well back out. Now that the concept had been broached he would indeed appear to be completely selfish if he nixed it. On the other hand, Sam didn't get the impression that the man had an altruistic bone in his body. He seemed like the type who, given unlimited money, would keep adding to his acquisitions—another house or two, a yacht or plane, world travel. She got a thrill out of watching him squirm.

"Rupert, I think we should cap off this lovely afternoon by examining the art. You shall have first selection of the piece you'd like for your own collection. Then, if everyone is in agreement, I shall choose the pieces that deserve to be hung at the new place." Sam saw a panicky look go between Bart and Carolyn. Maybe she'd overstepped in her role as the rich woman who routinely got her way. "Of course, there will be time for all that."

"The champagne!" said Carolyn Hildebrandt.

"Yes—let's." Bart recovered enough to realize that the whole thing had slipped out of his control. He stepped forward and ushered everyone away from the safe room and out of his study.

Sam found herself taking tiny sips of the sparkling wine, claiming that she had a long drive ahead. Rupert continued his role with ease, chatting on about the paintings and going so far as to walk back to the safe, move the canvases about until he could see them all, and proceed to choose one to buy. He even peeled a few hundred dollars off and handed it to Bart as a deposit.

What had just happened in there?

Walking out of the house, Sam felt as if she had nails in her clothing and tacks in her shoes. Acting was definitely not her forte, she decided as they rode back to the gallery with Carolyn Hildebrandt and said their goodbyes. She took a moment in Rupert's vehicle, to write down the names of the paintings on which she'd seen the green residue, so she could report them accurately to Beau. The prickly feeling began to subside as they got away from Santa Fe.

By the time they cruised north through Velarde, she was dozing lightly in the car. She roused as they approached Taos, straightening in her seat and half wondering whether she'd dreamed Rupert's dramatic little scene at Killington's house. But the crumpled piece of paper in her hand reminded her that she still had to report her findings to Beau.

Kelly's car was in the driveway when Rupert dropped Sam off at her house.

"How was your day with Iris?" Sam asked.

"It was good. Just getting used to being with one person all day."

Sam looked over at her daughter, who was busy stirring cocoa powder into a mug. She didn't detect anything wrong.

"Oh, Beau said to tell you to give him a call," Kelly said. She gave a lopsided grin. "I think he's going to ask you out."

Sam caught herself blushing.

"Mom . . . what's with the getup?"

Sam glanced down and remembered she was still dressed in the Mrs. Knightly gear. "Uh, Rupert and I went to this art thing."

"Oh."

Sam hurried to her room and changed into comfortable flannels and then returned Beau's call. They made plans for dinner the following evening and he laughingly assured her that she wouldn't have to wear hiking boots this time.

They met at the restaurant, a Mexican place just off Highway 64, convenient for her since she'd spent part of the afternoon checking on her ski-valley area property. She'd needed the physical exertion of chopping at underbrush to work off her frustration after the buyer of her truck called to say that he had to cancel. Just couldn't put the money together. The pickup once again sported its For Sale sign and Rupert assured Sam there was no hurry in repaying him.

Beau had asked Kelly to do a little evening duty, to stay

and give Iris dinner and get her settled in for the night. Sam found herself watching for clues as he talked, but everything Beau said about Kelly's job performance sounded positive. Apparently she'd begun to form a solid friendship with Iris, and Beau seemed very happy with the arrangement.

A waiter brought margaritas and took their food orders.

Once they got all the chitchat out of the way, Sam broached the other subject that was on her mind.

"Rupert and I took a drive to Santa Fe yesterday. He's trying to spearhead a move to set up a memorial to Cantone, out at the property where he lived. He thinks Bart should sell a painting or two to finance it." She caught herself smiling at the memory. "Actually, he's laying a pretty heavy guilt trip on Bart for the undignified burial."

"Good. It really was a pretty crummy thing to do, seeing how well-loved Cantone was."

Their plates arrived just then, chile rellenos for Sam and a huge cheese-smothered beef burrito for Beau. They spent a couple of minutes taking the first bites and exclaiming over the good, hot chile before Sam turned the conversation back to art.

"There are fourteen paintings at Bart's house. I saw green smudges on six of them. Interesting that not all of them had it. And I watched the others carefully. No one else apparently saw any of it."

"Remember that I told you we had a print expert trying to get something usable from Cantone's body. He was able to get viable prints from the palm of one hand and some partial prints of two fingers."

"I'm sensing a 'but,' " Sam said.

"But nothing matched. Not one of those plant residue smudges matched with anything we got from Cantone."

"They don't match Cantone and they don't match Bart?" Her fork clattered against the plate.

"Right."

"So now what?"

"Someone else was in that house. Someone who handled both the poisonous plant and the paintings." He paused for another bite of his burrito.

"Have you had the chance to question the neighbors yet?"

He shook his head. "I think I have some more questions for Mr. Bart Killington, though."

Sam had a discouraging feeling that she knew how that would turn out. Maybe she would try to talk again with Betty McDonald, and perhaps Leonard Trujillo, herself.

They shared an apple cobbler for dessert, with a nice wine, and Beau began to get that certain look in his eye again. When he suggested, "your place?" she knew she was ready.

She gave the living room a critical look as they walked in, wishing she'd planned ahead, thought to neaten up the place, to have some candles ready, to chill some wine. But in the end, it didn't matter. Beau took her into his arms and her insides went molten as they kissed.

She took him to her bedroom and switched on a small lamp. They undressed quickly and found a mutual rhythm of desire.

Later, as they lay together, he traced a line over her shoulder. "You're magical," he said.

She glanced past him, to the wooden box on the dresser. She hadn't touched it all day. Any magic tonight had come strictly on her own.

Chapter 27

Beau left around midnight and Sam snuggled into her covers. Her body felt alive, sparkling with the combination of great sex, the wine they'd shared after the first time, then the second leisurely exploration of each other. She savored the feeling. She had memories of younger times, other lovers, but nothing like this. Beau satisfied more than her physical needs—he gave emotionally, in a way she would treasure. The years of self-enforced celibacy seemed a little silly now.

At some point she heard Kelly come in but she registered the sound only as a vague fact, an event without the power to intrude into her dreams. She fell into a deep, pleasant sleep.

The faraway sound of the telephone woke Sam and she rolled over to glance at her clock. It was well after nine. Kelly had probably gotten up and left for work almost two hours ago. Sam pulled on a robe and caught the phone just before the answering machine took over.

"Hey you." Beau's tone indicated that he was alone somewhere. "How are you this morning?"

"Completely luxuriating in a lazy morning."

"Good. You deserve it. That was amazing last night."

She agreed. "Are you at work?"

"Yeah, actually. Couldn't get out of it. Although I would've loved to." Again, that ache in his voice.

Sam remembered that she had work she couldn't avoid either. The book cake for the Chocoholics was baked but not decorated. She would have to get it to the store by this afternoon. And she hadn't worked on Cantone's place in several days. With the recent rains and warm weather, she ought to see if the yard needed another mowing. She didn't tell him about her idea of talking to the neighbors out there.

"I'm having Bart Killington brought up here for more questioning," Beau was saying. "He may not be a suspect anymore, but he knows more than he's telling. Maybe I can find out who the other person was, the one handling the deathcamas."

"You don't have to go to Santa Fe for that?"

"If necessary, Sheriff Padilla can have the Santa Fe County authorities pick him up and bring him here. I think I've finally impressed upon him that we don't have a simple accidental death here. Getting Bart away from his own territory might help throw a little fear into him. Make him more talkative. Who knows? He may come willingly." Some papers rustled in the background. "I've got about a dozen reports to finish up, but maybe we can get together later in the day, or this evening?"

Sam agreed and wished him luck, already preoccupied

with her own duties for the day. By the time she'd dressed and grabbed a piece of toast for breakfast, she was feeling the pressure to get the cake done. She quickly iced it with milk chocolate buttercream, piped borders around the edges, then wrote the words "It was a dark and stormy night . . ." in dark chocolate script on the right-hand 'page' of the book shape. For the left side, roses seemed too traditional so she made mounds of tiny flowers in white chocolate that became clusters of hydrangeas. She added dark chocolate stems and leaves, and strategically sprinkled dragées and edible chocolate glitter to catch the light. That final step made the entire cake practically glow.

Sam looked at it with satisfaction. She felt almost the same radiance, herself.

She popped the cake into the fridge to set while she cleaned up the mess in the kitchen. A tuna sandwich and baggie full of potato chips would serve as lunch, sometime between delivering the cake and mowing Cantone's yard. The room darkened slightly, a cloud passing across the face of the sun, heralding a shift away from their warm Indian Summer days.

A subtle chill sneaked down her spine when she thought of Cantone. Beau's words came back. He would be questioning Bart Killington today. Why did that suddenly bother her?

Sam shook off the feeling and changed to work clothes. As she put her good gold hoop earrings into the wooden box, it sent its familiar warmth into her hands. She hadn't realized that they were cold as ice.

She held the box an extra minute, her hands absorbing the heat they needed. When she set it down again she felt her energy return. She paused a moment to let it surge through her, welcoming the power she would put to good use in accomplishing her tasks.

The white van waited in the driveway beside the Silverado. Soon, she told herself. Soon she would get signs made and Sweet's Sweets would become a presence as she drove around town. Briefly debating which vehicle to take, she couldn't resist driving the new one. She set the cake carefully in the back, hitched up the trailer with her lawn equipment and started rolling.

As always, Ivan Petrenko was effusive in his praise of the new dessert for the Chocoholics.

"Is reading a gothic mystery this week, for the group," he said. He showed her the book. "See? 'Dark and stormy night' is perfect motif. How do you know?"

How, indeed? Sam shrugged it off and wished him well.

By the time she reached Cantone's property heavy clouds had begun to build over the mountains. She stared upward and gave a nervous chuckle. The changing weather must be the real reason for her 'dark and stormy' inspiration.

Beyond Cantone's property the house belonging to Leonard Trujillo, the property boundary complainer, looked empty with no vehicles in the driveway. Betty McDonald's place looked similarly unoccupied. Later, Sam thought, she could catch them and ask questions after she finished her work.

She lowered the short ramp on the trailer and pulled the mower to the ground as the dark cloud moved closer. Wet grass wouldn't cut well; she should get it done before trying to question the neighbors anyway. The machine started right up and she made quick work of the areas in front of the house. A patch of the scary deathcamas grew near the steps to the porch and she cut it down without a second thought. Zoe's description of its effects, the violent convulsing death, haunted her. As the shredded stems flew away from the mower Sam felt an almost physical ache for poor Pierre Cantone.

Dark gray clouds covered most of the sky now.

She steered the mower to the backyard, making a perimeter where the lawn's edge touched the wild grasses and sage beyond. As she passed the dark hole in the earth, where the sheriff's men had dug up the artist's body, she again felt that slice of fear up her spine. What had the old man gone through as he ingested the poison, day after day, slowly dying. Did he know he would end up in this corner, covered by the heaps of soil that now lay in dark piles?

She turned her back, aiming the mower in the opposite direction.

Calm down, Sam, she told herself. What's the matter with you?

A flash of lightning in the distance caught her attention. Great. She pushed the mower a little faster. Doubling back, she concentrated on the work, on making neat rows and refusing to think about Cantone or his death.

The first drops of rain began to smack the earth. From the depth of the black clouds overhead, Sam knew her work was coming to a halt. She cut the mower's engine and steered toward the covered carport.

That's when she spotted the plume of dust. A dark vehicle roared along the road, kicking up dirt. Someone trying to beat the storm to get home. But as she watched, the shape became a green Jaguar and the car whipped into the driveway right behind her van.

Chapter 28

They say you should never kick a wasp's nest. Sam knew that, from the time she was a little girl. From the moment she watched the Jag roar to a halt in front of the house, she knew that the kick had been sent and that the nest was blazing with fury.

Bart Killington flung the door open, jumped out and slammed it shut behind him.

"You bitch!" he screamed.

Sam kept the lawnmower between them. "Excuse me?"

"You started this. *You* sent my life straight to hell!" Thunder crashed, punctuating his statement.

"I don't know what you mean." He'd found out. He'd figured out the Mrs. Knightly charade. Knew about her finding the poisonous plants.

"You are connected to that deputy in some way. He thought he'd haul me up here in handcuffs, didn't he?

Thought he'd found his suspect. Well, listen, bitch. It's not me! I came up here of my own free will, to try to help. But all he wants is to find somebody to blame. To take away my inheritance and make me suffer."

"Bart, calm down."

She might as well have invited him to rant on. He continued to scream, louder. She glanced around, hoping that one of the absent neighbors might come by and stop to check it out. Even if one of them were home the other houses were too far away and the rolling thunder was almost constant now.

A bolt of lightning struck an open field across the road, less than a quarter mile away. Every hair on her body stood on end. She jumped away from the metal lawnmower, standing near the walkway to the front porch. If she could just get inside and lock the door . . .

Bart stood in the open, daring the lightning, oblivious to the rain that now came down in sheets and pasted his dark hair to his scalp. His eyes were wild.

Another crash—this time somewhere behind the house.

Sam ran for the front door. Realized too late that it was still locked.

By the time she pulled the key from her pocket Bart was right beside her. The roof over the small porch provided no protection and Sam felt the rain soak her cotton work shirt. She dashed back to the cover of the carport, keeping an eye on Bart as he followed her.

"Bart, calm down." She reached out to touch his arm. He recoiled as if she'd punched him and backed two steps away from her.

"I'm not giving up the money from the paintings," he

said. His voice took on a plaintive note. "My uncle left them to me. I came here and stayed with him, took care of him when he was sick."

Sick from being poisoned. Sam watched his face carefully as he spoke. Was he actually so deluded as to think that he was doing his uncle a service as he slowly poisoned him to death?

Movement on the road grabbed Sam's attention. A dark vehicle slithered sideways on the wet, muddy road then corrected and picked up speed. Losing traction again, it came at the driveway almost sideways and slid to a stop behind Bart's Jaguar. Carolyn Hildebrandt leaped out.

Her eyes were intense and ropes of dark hair blew across her face. She grabbed at the strands, pushing them aside, but the wind and blowing rain pasted the hair against her cheeks again.

"Bart!" she shouted.

He turned, finally noticing.

"Bart! What are you doing?" Carolyn advanced on them.

Bart glanced back at Sam. "I didn't hurt him. I swear I didn't."

Sam almost believed him, could see what Beau meant about Bart's convincing manner.

"Bart, you fool! I *knew* I couldn't trust you not to talk to the cops," Carolyn shouted. "I *knew* I'd have to stop you!" She raised a pistol.

Sam froze.

Her mind went into overdrive. What did she have for defense? A lawnmower? She desperately tried to come up with a plan but her thoughts ricocheted about, refusing to focus.

"Okay, I wanted the paintings," Bart babbled. "I wanted the money. I knew they were valuable and my uncle was doing nothing with them but letting them hang in this pitiful little dump. I tried to sneak one out of the house and sell it, but he noticed it was gone."

"Bart . . ." Carolyn stood at the edge of the driveway, the pistol pointing right at them. "Shut up."

"She told me we could make a lot of money," he whined.

Sam muttered under her breath. "Maybe you better quit talking, Bart." She couldn't take her eyes off Carolyn.

"Bart, I'm warning you." Carolyn walked a little closer.

"Sweetheart, don't do anything," Bart said. "Let's just leave. Go back to my place."

Movement on the road caught Sam's attention for a second.

"You dumb fool," Carolyn hissed. "I can't believe how stupid you are."

Bart's eyes hardened. "Wait a minute—you didn't think I was so stupid when I led you right to a valuable collection of Cantone's work. You didn't think I was stupid when I let you start selling them. Carolyn—we *love* each other."

Sam held her breath. The vehicle approaching on the road was Beau's cruiser. She willed herself not to look that direction as he coasted up to the driveway, blocking Carolyn's vehicle.

"You're more idiotic than you'll ever know," Carolyn said. "You actually thought I *loved* you? You didn't have a clue that the only reason I stayed with you in this . . . this *shack* was because I saw that you'd never take what was yours. You would wait *years* for your uncle to die. And even then you didn't *know* that he'd leave his work to you. I had to make up that will and forge his signature. You would have never taken any real action. You're the kind who sits around and hopes life will turn out the way he wants it to. I—*I'm* the one who makes things happen."

The green fingerprints, Sam realized. *Carolyn's.*

Beau was out of his vehicle now and Sam saw him slowly approach. She was the only one who could see him, and it took a force of will not to stare, not to let her relief show on her face.

Sam's attention went back to Carolyn. The art dealer's expression was pure rage. The woman clearly had gone over the edge and Sam suddenly realized that she had no intention of letting Bart or Sam out of here alive. Again, she raised the pistol, her finger firmly on the trigger. The only minuscule bit of hesitation seemed to come from the decision about which of them to shoot first. Her eyes darted from one to the other.

Make an impossible target, Sam told herself. She spun toward Bart and shoved him to the left, while she dove for the ground in the opposite direction. She hit, rolled, and came up at the edge of the carport as the shot reverberated.

Bart lay huddled in a ball against the wall of the house but Sam couldn't see any blood. Carolyn's shot had gone wild, the bullet smacking into one of the carport's wooden supports.

The woman had a wild look in her eyes as she spun toward Bart, taking aim once more.

"Freeze!" Beau shouted. His own pistol was out now, his two-handed grip looking very firm.

Carolyn fired again. Sam heard the ricochet and chips of concrete sprayed near Bart. Then Carolyn turned on Beau.

His shot went unhesitatingly, right into her shoulder. She dropped her own gun and slumped to the ground. He kicked her gun aside and kept his aimed at her.

"Stay right there," he said. He keyed his shoulder mike and called for backup and an ambulance.

Sam felt relief rush through her body. She met Beau's gaze and sent him a tentative smile. He winked. It was going to be okay.

Chapter 29

The thunderstorm cleared as quickly as it had come on, typical of early autumn storms near the mountains. Beau's backup officer arrived about ten minutes later. As the ambulance made its way back toward town with Carolyn Hildebrandt strapped to a gurney inside, Sam went into Cantone's house and found some old towels. Blotting much of the residual wetness from her own hair and clothing, she offered another towel to Beau.

"How did you know I was in trouble?" she asked.

He pulled a blanket from his cruiser and draped it over Bart Killington's shoulders. Handcuffs bound Bart's hands. He sat with his back to the wall of the house, white-faced and shaking, unmoving since Beau had read him his rights and placed him under arrest for grand theft, conspiracy to commit murder, and fraud.

Beau stared hard at the prisoner. "I didn't. I just happened to look out the window after I'd questioned this jerk. Saw him rush out to his car. Something about the look on his face. During the interview he'd begun raging about how much trouble all this had caused him. I got a bad feeling. I planned on following him to the south end of Taos, just to make sure he left town, but when he headed this direction and I knew you were here . . ."

"But—Carolyn?"

"I never saw her. Got hung up with a fender-bender in town, had to radio Taos police to handle it." He pulled Sam into his embrace. "I was pretty worried that I'd gotten too far behind him."

Sam leaned against his chest. His timing couldn't have been better.

"I'm going to have about a week's worth of paperwork to do," Beau murmured, keeping an eye on his prisoner. "But I want to see you this evening. If you're up to some kind of take-out dinner and a few drinks."

She was more than up for it. A quiet evening at home seemed like nirvana at that moment. She watched as Beau led Killington to the cruiser and secured him in the back seat. The backup officer continued to photograph the places where Carolyn's bullets left their mark, and to bag the gun and the smashed bullet from the carport post.

The late-afternoon sun was already doing its work at drying the road and droplets of water clinging to the newly clipped grass provided only a small reminder of the ferocity of the storm. In the flowerbeds beside the house a few late roses shed beaten petals, their final act before winter. The head of one deathcamas, however, bloomed as heartily as ever, protected by an overhanging rosebush.

Sam locked the front door and watched Beau drive away. A few minutes later, the other officer finished and went on his way. Sam surveyed the property that had been under her care for the past two weeks. It seemed lonelier than ever.

Chapter 30

Nine messages waited on Sam's machine when she got home, with another five on her cell phone, which she'd left in the van all afternoon. Among them were Rupert (twice), Zoe, Ivan Petrenko, and a couple other friends. Even Kelly and Iris had heard the story on the news before Beau got the chance to call home and reassure his mother. Some zealous reporter had caught the police call on the scanner and was waiting with cameras rolling when Beau led Bart Killington into the county jail for booking.

Exterior shots of the hospital at which "an unknown woman with a gunshot wound" was admitted were what prompted all the calls to Sam. Apparently Rupert, the only one who knew enough of the story to put it together, had gone a little off the deep end with worry and had begun calling around to see if Sam were with friends. When she wasn't, they all assumed the worst. Zoe and Darryl had actually driven to the hospital, only to learn that the injured woman was someone else.

Sam spent two hours returning calls and explaining before she finally decided enough was enough. She wanted a hot shower and a cup of tea.

Beau showed up an hour later, bringing Kelly and Iris, and they sat down for pizza and beer. He told them that Carolyn's injury was only serious enough to warrant one night's hospital stay at county expense. She would be taken to jail the next day and booked for first degree murder, grand theft and a bunch more things.

Bart had apparently jabbered away all afternoon, telling how Carolyn had begun gathering this plant that she told Bart was an herbal remedy for insomnia, which the older man had suffered for years. One of them would make him a cup of tea with it each evening. Bart claimed that he never made the connection between the plant and his uncle's increasing illness.

Sam remembered seeing books on botany on the shelves in Carolyn's gallery, during her first visit in Mrs. Knightly mode. The woman knew exactly what she was doing.

"We'll see what the jury believes," Beau said. "I have a feeling Carolyn is going to put a whole different spin on the story."

Chapter 31

Sam gave herself the luxury of doing absolutely nothing the next day. She slept through Kelly's leaving for Beau's house that morning, drank tea and read a book until Zoe stopped by to see if she wanted to go out for lunch. They ate quiche and salads at a little café on Bent Street, lingering at the table until mid-afternoon. By four o'clock Sam began to feel impatient with the unaccustomed leisure so she went home and sat at the kitchen table, making a to-do list.

The quinceañera cake was the only large order on the horizon, so she had some spare time for fall housecleaning and smaller projects. She wrote down everything she wished to accomplish, knowing that she'd be doing well to get half of it done. Closets, drawers and pantry could all use cleanout and organization. Bedding should be laundered. Windows washed. Garden trimmed and mulched. Garage—she almost didn't even want to go there.

As she toured the house, remembering each little task,

her gaze fell on the wooden box. Would it hurt to call upon its power? The extra energy she drew from it could be used to her advantage . . . No. She stopped herself. Somehow it didn't seem wise to count on the box for every little thing. Starting to use its power for mundane chores like housework didn't feel right. She turned her back on it.

Thursday morning Sam awoke full of vigor, without the need for help from the wooden box. After a quick breakfast she baked the tiers for the quinceañera cake and set them to cool. While the cakes were in the oven she whipped up buttercream frosting and tinted it in batches. Those set aside, she went into her room, stripped the bedding and started a load of laundry.

While I'm at it I might as well turn the mattress, she decided. She'd upended the queen-size piece when she realized there was something under it.

Cantone's sketchbook. She'd forgotten all about placing it there for safe keeping.

She took it out, rearranged the mattress and sat down. The crisp pages contained small vignettes that she recognized from some of his work. A gazebo that he'd rendered in gray and white; a wicker chair, done in green and dappled with sunlight in another painting. Sam flipped through the sketches, admiring them with a new perspective. Who owned all this? she wondered. Now that Carolyn had admitted to faking the will Sam found at Bart's house, and if Bart went to prison for his role . . .

The answer fell, literally, into her lap.

The sheaf of legal-sized sheets were stapled at the top with a blue cover sheet. Atop that, a business card. A New York telephone number. She glanced at it quickly then lifted the cover sheet.

The Last Will and Testament of Pierre Cantone . . .

Sam read quickly, scanning back over occasional passages couched in legalese. It was all here—legal and airtight—dated ten years ago. Cantone had set up a trust, leaving all his possessions to the Etheridge, a small New York museum. His stated reason for the choice was that he felt his work would receive the attention it deserved with the personal care of the museum director, rather than being entrusted to one of the larger places that vied for the works of great numbers of artists.

Sam remembered Rupert telling her that Cantone's reputation had been hard-won. Too many of the large museums and the critics of his early years had been harsh with him. Perhaps that was the real reason he shunned them at the end of his life.

How close they'd come to never knowing this will existed. Cantone must have hidden the sketchbook inside the wall when he began to suspect that Bart was trying to raid the estate. He could have simply called his attorney and made the contents public in order to thwart his nephew, but who knew how muddled his thinking might have become as he got sicker and sicker.

She ran her hand over one of the small color sketches in his book, feeling a connection with the man who'd worked so hard to please the art world while remaining true to his soul as an artist. She felt a prickle at her eyelids.

Now she needed to know what to do. With a sigh she closed the sketchbook and carried the legal document to the kitchen. She dialed the attorney's number.

Chapter 32

October gold. With the first days of the new month, chill New Mexico nights had turned the landscape to every shade of amber, orange, yellow and ocher. Like a Cantone painting come alive, the view from his property held the magical light that gained the artist his reputation in life. Now, in death, the great man would have his wish— to lie forever in the spot that held his heart, to become a permanent part of the land he loved.

Sam stood at the edge of the gathering, among friends. Reflecting on the man, the artist. It turned out that Bart had not been too far off the mark in his choice for his uncle's remains. Cantone had, indeed, specified in his will that he wanted to be buried on the land, here in New Mexico.

His attorney knew the artist's wishes well. He immediately contacted the Etheridge Museum and set the wheels in motion. Their representatives arrived in Taos that morning. Rupert's friend, Esteban, had even flown in from

New York—the man who'd originally identified the mural as Cantone's work which started the whole investigation. He'd brought the mural with him and it would soon be back in place in the closet wall where Cantone painted it.

Sam glanced around at the assembled crowd. Rupert, Zoe and Darryl, Beau, Iris and Kelly—they all hovered around her, knowing that standing here at the graveside was difficult. She would need to reassure them, again, that she was fine. The burial site had been properly dug to the right depth this time, the simple wooden coffin reflected the artist's unadorned lifestyle, and a marble tombstone would forever mark the spot. After the service, wildflowers would be planted on the grave, an assortment that would assure almost year-round blooms.

The museum director had been chosen to officiate since Cantone was known to be non-religious. He clearly would have been happy with the choice, as the man spoke in reverent tones about the dedication that Cantone gave to his life's work, holding up the sketchbook to illustrate certain points. Few knew that the artist had used money from the sales of his earliest works to fund an art school in Provence, or that he'd regularly painted small items which he donated to charity auctions. Sam felt a warm glow as she realized how much the artist had contributed, knowing that she had some part in seeing that he would be properly remembered.

To her right, Rupert was weeping openly. Across the open grave the other staffers from the Etheridge stood with bowed heads, handkerchiefs in hand.

". . . he will live in our memories forever." The director closed the book. Thus concluded, the mourners began to drift away, toward the house. Sam's final tribute to the artist—a cake depicting the open sketchbook with a few of his unknown drawings rendered in frosting—waited inside, where the guests would share it, along with tea and memories.

"Sam, might I speak with you a moment?" the museum director said as they walked toward the house. "Privately."

They stepped aside and let the others pass by. A cool breeze glided over her arms as they stood in the shadow of the house.

"I've been in touch with the authorities," he said, "and I'm assured that the large house Bart Killington bought with money he illegally obtained from the estate is now ours. We will place that house on the market immediately and use the proceeds to pay the mortgage on this property. It should be sufficient for most of the renovations, as well."

"So you won't need to sell paintings for that?"

"Correct. As I understand it, Mr. Killington will most likely be living in the care of the State for quite a few years."

He continued: "Cantone's house will be renovated for structural integrity and his simple furniture will remain. The back bedroom can be redone as the great artist's studio, giving visitors a glimpse into the life and work of the man. And of course, we will spare no expense to outfit the house with the best security system possible and to provide staff so it can be open as a visitor's center year-round. The estate provides money for that."

"I'm so glad," Sam told him. "From the moment I stumbled upon the grave, and then learned who lived here, I felt sad about there being such a depressing end for this talented man."

"As we become more familiar with the trust Cantone created, and learn how much we have in the way of funds," he said, "we want to do more to promote the arts here. One of our thoughts would be to build a secondary building on the site, a place for an art school. I'm sure there will be adequate money for it."

Sam felt the tears threaten again. "That would be so nice. Thank you."

She started to turn toward the house.

"Samantha, there is one more thing."

She stopped and faced him.

"The sketchbook. Without you, it would have never been found."

She waved off the praise. "A lucky find, for sure."

"We feel that it belongs to you. As a reward for everything you've done."

"But, I—I really didn't do anything."

"No, my dear. Think of it. You found the mural. It led to the sketchbook. You contacted the right people to identify the paintings and that became the beginning of our learning where Cantone had been all these years. Not to mention that you located the correct will. Without you, we might have never learned what a benefactor he was to us. It was an immensely important find."

She smiled at him. "I suppose it was."

"It's yours." He held up the sketchbook but didn't hand it over. "And now that I've given it, might I make a suggestion?"

Puzzled, she cocked her head.

"We have already been contacted by a collector, a woman who is probably the most avid fan of Cantone in the world.

She has heard word of the book and would like to buy it."

Sam hesitated. She loved the book, loved looking at the artist's sketches.

"This woman, you must understand, knew Cantone in his younger years. She . . . how do I say this delicately? . . . she probably was his lover, lived with him, in those dark times after his wife died. Most likely, she watched him with pencil in hand as he made many of those sketches."

"Oh. Then you are absolutely right. She should have it." Sam took a step back.

"I had a feeling you might say that." He reached into the inside pocket of his jacket. "That's why I accepted this on your behalf."

He pulled out a long white envelope and handed it to Sam.

"What's this?" She pried up the flap. Inside was a check with so many zeros in the figure that it took her breath away.

"It—it's too much. I can't take this." She started to hand it back but he raised his palm.

"But— How can it be—"

"The book is worth it to her. And she's a woman who can afford it. Trust me."

"But—what about the visitor's center, the art school? Wouldn't it be better spent there?"

"I've already told you, we have plenty for those projects. We want you to have this. Surely there's something you can use the money for?"

Her eyes welled up. "Yes, there is something I've dreamed of for a very long time." And she knew the perfect location. The tears spilled, dripping off her chin. "I'll put it to good use."

He pulled a handkerchief from his pocket and dabbed at her face while she stood there helplessly. "Come, my dear. Let's have some of that beautiful cake you made."

What's Next For Samantha Sweet?

Sam's dream of opening her own pastry shop is coming true, but in the midst of opening Sweet's Sweets Sam finds herself caught up in another mystery.

Among the items Sam has carted off to the thrift shop from one of her break-in jobs is a heavily blood-stained garment that raises a lot of questions. The sheriff's department takes over but the clues are elusive. Sam's new man, Deputy Sheriff Beau Cardwell, has a tough time convincing his boss to treat the coat as evidence of a murder—it's an election year and Sheriff Padilla doesn't want bad press before he's securely back in office.

But Sam has other tools at her disposal. The wooden box which came into her possession weeks earlier seems to give her the ability to see beyond the obvious. And when she begins to get strong impressions about some of the guests at her store's grand opening gala, she figures out which course Beau should take in the investigation. Things heat up from all directions as Sam and Beau begin to work out the puzzle.

Ask for it at your favorite bookstore or find it online at most major book retailers.

Sweet's Sweets
The Second Samantha Sweet Mystery
by Connie Shelton

Connie Shelton is the author of the *USA Today* bestselling Charlie Parker mysteries, the Samantha Sweet mystery series and a new series of adventure books for kids. She has taught writing—both fiction and nonfiction—and is the creator of the Novel In A Weekend™ writing course. She lives in northern New Mexico with her husband and two dogs.

Sign up for Connie's free email mystery newsletter and get announcements of new books, discount coupons, and the chance for some 'sweet' deals.

www.connieshelton.com

CPSIA information can be obtained
at www.ICGtesting.com
Printed in the USA
LVOW13s2224170117
521309LV00013B/669/P